CRUEL DECEPTION

JEANETTE BURNS

Published 2024 by Your Book Angel
Copyright © Jeanette Burns

All rights reserved. No part of this book may be reproduced, stored, or transmitted by any means—whether auditory, graphic, mechanical, or electronic—without written permission of both publisher and author, except in the case of brief excerpts used in critical articles and reviews. Unauthorized reproduction of any part of this work is illegal and is punishable by law.

The characters are all mine, any similarities with other fictional or real persons/places are coincidental.

Printed in the United States
Edited by Keidi Keating
Layout by Rochelle Mensidor

ISBN: 979-8-9897121-6-8

Chapter One

Ada Claridge sat in the library looking out the window, reliving everything that had gone wrong. It seemed to be all she did lately. Her parents' divorce had been the talk of the town for weeks. Despite her father's efforts to keep it out of the gossip columns, word had rapidly spread among the upper class.

Ada knew her parents' divorce would hurt her standing in society, although she didn't expect it to ruin her. But it happened anyway when rumors were spread about her having sexual relations with Malcolm Randolph.

It was bad enough that her mother was in exile, leaving Ada alone, but now she couldn't even bring herself to leave the house. The last time she'd left was to go shopping.

She hadn't expected to run into her former friends while she was out, but had put on a brave face when their paths crossed at the dressmaker's shop. She'd smiled through gritted teeth, unsurprised when probing questions about her relationship with Randolph were asked. Of course she denied the rumors, but with her mother gone, she had no protection from the ton.

Veronica Aldridge had been there, much to Ada's chagrin. Surprisingly, Veronica had invited her to tea, making it clear to everyone present that she was willing to associate with Ada in spite of what had happened. Ada was shocked that Veronica would help her after everything she had done. She wondered if Veronica's invitation was genuine, or merely a ruse intended to further humiliate her. Only time would tell.

The plot Ada's mother, Agnes, had derived would have ruined Veronica and destroyed her life. Ada had been a willing participant in the plot, and this was something she now deeply regretted. The irony of how the plan had backfired was not lost on Ada.

Growing up, Ada always got what she wanted. Guided and shaped by her calculating mother, she'd grown into a self-centered, manipulative young woman. Having captured the heart of Owen Pierce, son of the esteemed Lord Calum Pierce, Earl of Westridge, she'd known it was only a matter of time before he proposed. Ada had believed Owen's family was as affluent as her own, and that she and Owen were the perfect match. But when Owen confided that his family had lost their fortune, Ada immediately sought her mother's counsel.

Threatening to expose the Pierce family's secret, Agnes convinced Owen's mother, Ann, to agree to a secret arrangement that would see Owen marry Veronica instead of Ada. Owen had vehemently opposed the plan at first, but eventually agreed to it, with the understanding he could eventually divorce Veronica and marry Ada.

Owen despised the idea of hurting Veronica, but Ada had persuaded him it was the only way they could be together. What she omitted to tell Owen was her mother's scheme to have Veronica's reputation compromised by Malcolm Randolph. The plan had ultimately failed, and in the end, it was Ada who suffered the most.

Since then, Ada had spent a lot of time reflecting on her life. About the things she had done and the horrible person she had become. She wondered if her father would ever truly forgive her. He was the one person she had left, now that her mother had abandoned her. She was so lost in thought, she did not hear the door open behind her.

* * *

Lord Thomas stood in the doorway, staring at his daughter. He'd been so preoccupied with his own affairs that he had not paid any attention to her emotional state. As he looked at her now, he was stunned. Ada had always been a vain girl who did not leave her room until she looked her best. Now she was her wearing what appeared to be a maid's dress, and her hair was unbrushed and needed washing. He felt sick, realizing his daughter was suffering and he had not noticed.

"Ada," he said softly.

Ada looked up, startled. She watched her father as he approached.

"Yes, father?" She asked.

"I have a surprise for you," he said. He walked over and handed her the letter he'd been holding.

Ada didn't reach for it. She was afraid of what it might say.

"It won't bite you," he said, smiling.

"Are you sure?" She asked, looking nervous.

"Yes. It's from Veronica," he answered.

Surprised, she looked at him, finally accepting the letter. She hurriedly opened it and scanned the contents.

"She invited me to tea tomorrow afternoon. I didn't believe she truly wanted to do this," Ada said after a moment. She continued to stare at the letter.

"That's good," her father said, gently sitting down beside her. His daughter looked conflicted. "What are you thinking?" He asked.

"Why would she be nice to me after everything I have done?" Ada asked.

"Her father, Lord Henry, told me she would reach out to you, and I asked him the same question. He told me his daughter does not hold grudges and will not take pleasure in somebody else's misery. She knows how you will be treated now and disapproves. It seems Veronica has never cared for what society deems appropriate. So, I think you should go."

"Maybe if you had married her mother, Ellen, I would have been a proper and decent lady," Ada said, looking at the floor.

"Nonsense," Thomas responded. "Veronica is like her birth mother, Leah. Ellen has been a great mother to her, but she is just like Leah."

"You knew her mother?" Ada asked, surprised.

"Yes. I, Henry, Callum, and Lord Archie Corbin met at Eton. We became friends and were inseparable. When Henry married Leah, it wasn't a love match. His father arranged it, and Henry was not pleased. His father was a mean bastard who threatened to disinherit him if he didn't go through with the marriage. Ellen was friends with Eleanor and a woman named Meredith, and they reached out to Leah. They became the best of friends."

Ada listened, happy for the distracting conversation. She noted that her father looked more relaxed than he had in a long time.

"Leah was sweet and giving, always helping people who needed it. She opened two orphanages and a house for women of ill repute to help give them a better life. Henry loves Ellen and is happy with her, but his feelings for Leah will never disappear. When Leah died, I thought he would never recover. I don't think he would have if it weren't for his children."

"I know Lady Eleanor Corbin. She is Veronica's friend, Hannah's mother, but who is Meredith?"

"I guess it is time to tell you why I divorced your mother," Thomas said with a sigh.

"It wasn't because of what we tried to do to Veronica?" Ada asked, surprised.

"Partly, but there was a more significant reason. Before I proposed to your mother, I was engaged to Meredith. She was the love of my life, in fact," Thomas stated.

Ada knew immediately that her mother must have done something. "What did mother do?" She asked.

"She hired someone to compromise Meredith in the worst way. Meredith's father was a Viscount and a hard man. He threw her out with nothing. I tried to find her even though my parents had stopped the engagement. If she had stayed, I would have run away with her to Gretna Green." Ada could see the pain on her father's face. She had heard of Gretna Green before. It was a place in Scotland where young couples could go to marry without the consent of their parents.

"You loved her that much to give up everything?" Ada asked, her eyes widening.

"Yes. I still do," he chuckled, seeing the astonished look on her face. "That surprises you?"

Ada's face became serious again. "I don't think I have ever felt that kind of love. Mother said love was not something a woman could afford to trust in. She told me station was all that I should concentrate on achieving," she said. Thomas looked at his daughter and wished he had given her a better mother. "And now I will be lucky to marry a pauper," she added, her eyes welling with tears.

"I don't want you to worry about finding a husband. Leave that to me. I will find a good man to marry you. Someone who will treat you right," Thomas said, smiling at his daughter.

"Thank you, father," said Ada as she leaned over to hug him.

"Now, go send Veronica a reply telling her you will meet her tomorrow," said Thomas.

"Yes father," Ada said dutifully. She stood up and left the library, looking a little less melancholy. Thomas watched her go, worry evident on his face.

* * *

Over the next few months, things settled down for Ada. People stopped talking about her, for she stayed out of sight, and other scandals took precedence. So, when the Carlyle annual ball came around, Thomas thought it the perfect opportunity to reintroduce his daughter to society.

"But father, it's too soon!" Protested Ada, when Thomas first broached the subject.

"Nonsense," said Thomas. "A ball is a wonderful way for you to reacquaint yourself with our friends. You may even attract the attention of a suitable young noble." When Ada remained unconvinced, he said, "You have a wardrobe full of beautiful gowns. Don't you want to dress up and feel pretty again?" Thomas searched for reasons that might appeal to his daughter.

"I don't want anyone to notice me," said Ada, sounding hesitant.

"You cannot hide yourself away indefinitely my dear," Thomas said finally, his tone firm.

"What if everyone still hates me?" Ada asked tearfully, realizing her father was adamant that she attend.

"They'll forgive you, just as I have," he answered confidently. "Everything will be fine, you'll see," he said. He left the room smiling, pleased the matter was resolved.

Ada watched her father leave, her eyes still bright with tears. He had no idea what he was asking of her. Although he may have forgiven her, she knew there were others who had not. Her transgressions would not be pardoned so easily by some. Retribution was inevitable, of that she was sure.

* * *

When Ada and Thomas entered the grand hall, their arrival was noted by everyone present. The people they passed stared and began whispering. Although her father appeared not to notice, Ada was well aware of the upset her presence had caused. Ada half hid behind her father, keeping her eyes down.

Viscount Anthony Carlyle stood in the corner talking to some friends when he caught sight of Lord Thomas Claridge, Earl of Kingsley. What held his attention, however, was the small thing hiding behind him. He had heard the scandal about Lord Thomas's daughter, but he was one who didn't let society dictate his life. He hated these social events and never attended them, but this one was an annual tradition of his family, so he had no choice. He didn't remember the young woman's name, but she reminded him of a frightened kitten, which bothered him.

Anthony had not wanted to talk to another woman since his wife, Genevieve, had died, taking his child with her. His heart had never recovered from the loss, and he believed it never would. But for some unknown reason, his eyes felt drawn to the young woman who so clearly did not want to be at his family's party that evening. He was puzzled by the protective instinct that welled up inside him as he looked at her. She was attractive to be sure, with rich chestnut hair and large brown eyes. Although petite, even from across the room he could still make out the womanly curves beneath her modest gown. Not that such things stirred him anymore. He did not understand why he felt such a strong urge to watch over the tiny creature and ensure nobody hurt her. *I simply wish to make sure nothing goes wrong this evening*, he told himself.

He relaxed when he saw Lady Ellen Cambridge, The Marquee of Cambridge, Henry Aldridge's wife, approach Lord Thomas's daughter and begin talking to her. He had business dealings with Henry and his son Ellis, and he knew Lady Ellen's character. She would never let anything happen to the young woman. With some effort, he turned his attention back to the conversation at hand.

* * *

"Hello, Ada. Glad to see you here this evening," Ellen said, smiling. "Good evening Lord Thomas," she added with a curtsy.

Ada looked up and smiled. "Good evening, Lady Ellen," she said shyly, dipping to curtsy.

"Good evening, Lady Ellen," Thomas responded with a gracious bow. He smiled warmly, pleased to see the kindness Ellen bestowed his daughter. "Did Henry come with you?" He asked.

"Yes, he is here somewhere, no doubt talking business," Ellen responded with a delicate wave of her gloved hand.

While Thomas and Ellen exchanged pleasantries, Ada took a moment to survey the vast room. Despite the fact all of society appeared to be in attendance, it still felt spacious. *Perhaps there's a private alcove or balcony where I can spend the remainder of the evening... Father won't notice my absence once he starts talking business with Lord Aldridge and the others*, she thought.

"Hello, Ada. I didn't notice you were here." The voice startled Ada from her thoughts. She looked around Ellen to see Charlotte Smitherman. Charlotte was one of Ada's friends—that is, she had been a friend until Ada's fall from grace. When the two had been friends, it was Charlotte who had instigated most of the torture dished out to girls she deemed lowly and beneath her. At the top of Charlotte's list had been Veronica Aldridge.

"There's more to being respected than who your father is," Charlotte used to say. This was how Charlotte justified her cruelty when she targeted Veronica. Even back then, Ada knew it was jealousy that motivated Charlotte, because Veronica was more of a lady than Charlotte would ever be.

"Hello, Charlotte," Ada said quietly. She searched Charlotte's face for signs of malice, but saw none. For the first time that evening, she began to feel hopeful.

Ellen stepped aside to make room for Charlotte. She continued chatting with Thomas, but kept an eye on Ada while the two girls spoke.

"I'm sorry I haven't reached out sooner," Charlotte said, sounding contrite. "You can understand the challenge... certain events of the past presented to someone of my station," she added. "Mother and father simply wouldn't hear of it when I asked permission to call on you." Charlotte looked genuinely regretful.

"Please don't apologize. I understand completely. It is in the past. And I am pleased for the chance to speak with you now," Ada said. *Was it possible Charlotte had suffered a change of heart after seeing what happened to me?* Ada wondered. Deciding everyone deserved a second chance, Ada began to let her guard down.

Moments later, two more of Ada's former friends approached and began talking to her as if nothing had happened.

"Ada, we've missed you," said Penelope.

"Your gown is divine. The white really sets off the blush of your cheeks," said Rose.

Ada began to relax as the other girls laughed and chatted with her.

"Why don't we avail ourselves of some punch. I am positively parched," suggested Charlotte.

Feeling thirsty as well, Ada agreed. "Some refreshments would be lovely," she said. Her father was still preoccupied with Lady Ellen, and didn't notice her leave his side.

"I'd love a little privacy so we can catch up properly," Charlotte said a few minutes later, as they withdrew from the refreshment table.

"I believe there's a quiet room down the hall," said Penelope.

"Okay, but only for a short while. Father might wonder where I am," said Ada.

"Don't worry, this won't take long," said Charlotte as she led the others rapidly down the hall.

Ada noticed the smiles the other girls exchanged. She felt lucky to have friends who were so forgiving.

Ellen noticed the girls as they exited the room, and felt a tug of misgiving. But Ada looked happy for the first time that evening. She watched as Ada trotted off after the trio. *Some time alone with friends is probably just what that poor girl needs,* she thought. But her feelings of doubt persisted.

* * *

"Are you so stupid as to think we would be friends with someone like you? A whore." Charlotte said as soon as the door to the private room closed behind them.

"Charlotte! Wha-what are you talking about? I—I thought—" Ada began, looking bewildered.

Before Ada could recover her composure, Charlotte slapped Ada hard enough to knock her to the floor. Ada clutched her face in shock. The other two girls moved quickly. With a sneer, Penelope poured her cup of ratafia over Ada's white dress. Next, Rose upended her plate, smashing the piece of cake it held onto Ada's head.

Blood leaked from Ada's mouth, and she felt her face swelling from the slap. Charlotte bent down to be at eye level with her.

"You need to keep away from polite society. You are not welcome here anymore. Good luck with finding a decent husband after being with Malcolm Randolph. You are disgusting," Charlotte said with vehemence. Ada cowered beside her. Not satisfied with the pain her words most surely inflicted, Charlotte quickly removed one of her gloves and reached out to grasp the top of Ada's dress. As she tore the fabric, her long, sharp fingernails left scratch marks on Ada's chest. Standing once more, she smirked at the pathetic girl sobbing before her.

"Ladies, shall we return to the festivities?" Charlotte asked as she donned her glove once more. No longer interested in their game, the three then left the room, laughing.

As the girls walk back inside the ballroom, Anthony noticed Ada was not with them. Concerned, he retraced their steps out to the corridor, checking all the rooms as he followed it to the end. Hearing muffled sobs through a door at the end of the hall, he knew his concern had been justified. "Lady Claridge, are you all right?" He asked, tapping urgently on the door. Receiving no response, he queried again. "It's Anthony Carlyle, my lady. I'm coming in," he said cautiously. Opening the door, Anthony was horrified to discover Ada weeping, still on the floor.

Ada raised her tear-streaked face in fear when she heard him call her name. *What else could those wretched girls have planned for me?* she wondered. Terrified, she crawled to the furthest corner and hid herself behind a large table. *Surely this gentleman with the kind eyes is not part of their vengeful plan*, she thought desperately.

Realizing the situation required both discretion and urgency, Anthony quickly withdrew from the room, shutting the door behind him. He called one of the servants over. "You. Stand before this door and let no one enter until I return," he commanded.

"Yes, my lord," answered the servant.

Returning to the ball, Anthony spotted Lady Ellen talking to Lady Eleanor. He walked over to where they stood. "Lady Aldridge," he said, nodding his head.

"Oh, Lord Carlyle, it's good to see you," said Lady Ellen.

"I require your assistance, but do not wish to cause a scene. There has been a young girl hurt," he said in a voice low enough that only the two ladies could hear him.

"Where?" asked Ellen, continuing to smile so it would appear they were simply having a friendly conversation.

"In one of the rooms. I will meet you in the corridor on the north side of the hall," Anthony said, casually gesturing to the left side of the room. At Ellen's nod, he bowed politely and walked back in the direction from which he'd come.

As soon as Anthony left, Ellen turned towards her friend. "Eleanor, I need you to walk with me. Act like nothing is out of the ordinary," she said.

The two ladies strolled towards the corridor, talking as if they were leaving the ball in search of a place to sit. Once outside the hall, they saw Anthony and walked to him.

"In here," he said, opening a door and stepping aside.

The two ladies entered the room and looked about. Puzzled, they looked at one another. Nobody was in there. "Where is she?" Ellen asked, turning towards Anthony. She paused and turned back to face the room when her ears caught the sound of a sniffle. Searching the room again, she realized the sound was coming from the vicinity of a table situated on the far wall. The table had an extended cover that touched the floor. Ellen crossed the room quietly, then bent down to lift the table covering. There lay Ada, curled against the wall, hiding her face.

"Ada?" Ellen said in a soft voice. Upon hearing her name, Ada tried to curl up even more. "Ada, sweetheart, it's Ellen. I'm not going to hurt you," she said gently. Ada slowly turned towards Ellen, revealing her swollen face and bloody mouth. Ellen's eyes widened with shock. "Come on, honey, let's get you out from under there," Ellen said, touching Ada's hand.

"I'm so sorry, so sorry. I never wanted to hurt anyone. I am truly sorry," Ada repeated as she cried even harder.

Anthony shut the door and stood by it to ensure no one else could enter the room.

"Honey, I know. It's okay. Come on out from under there. We can help you." Ellen said. She spoke reassuringly, trying to coax the frightened girl out from under the table. Ada slowly took Ellen's hand and allowed herself to be guided out. When Eleanor saw the state Ada was in, she began to tear up.

Anthony did not approach but he watched Ellen persuade Ada to come out from beneath the table. He was disturbed to see Ada's torn and stained dress, but rage engulfed him when he saw her face.

Eleanor crossed the room to join Ellen, swiftly surveying the damage done to Ada's dress. "I will go to the drawing room and see if I can find some pins," she said in a practical voice. She too was shaken, but she did not want the poor girl to see how upset she was. As walked towards the door, she paused in front of Anthony.

"Don't let anyone in; they might try to send people to further torment her," Eleanor said.

"Of that you need not worry," Anthony responded darkly. His eyes betrayed the depth of his anger. Eleanor nodded, satisfied, then glanced back at the girl now cradled in Ellen's arms before exiting the room.

On her way to retrieve the necessary items, Eleanor espied her daughter, Hannah.

"Mother, where have you been?" asked Hannah.

"Ellen and I are taking care of something. What are you doing out here unaccompanied?" Eleanor asked, changing the subject.

"I was just looking for you," Hannah answered, following her mother. "Dinah is departing for home and wondered if I could go with her," she asked.

"Certainly," answered Eleanor, stopping at the entrance of the drawing room. She was thankful she wouldn't have to tell Hannah what was happening. Kissing Hannah on the cheek, she sent her daughter on her way, then entered the room, retrieving several pins and some starched linen cloth from an ornately carved cabinet. Wasting no time, she quickly returned to the others, anxious to do what she could for Ada.

She knocked lightly on the door, and Anthony peeked out before opening it to let her in. Once inside, she walked over to a water pitcher and basin that had been brought in during her absence. Pouring some water into the basin, she wetted the cloths then brought them over to Ada.

"Ada, I need to clean your face. I know it will be tender, but it has to be done. All right?" Eleanor said softly.

Ada looked at Eleanor and slowly nodded, not saying anything as tears rolled down her face. Ellen had already removed the cake bits, and now began the process of re-pinning her hair. Ada flinched a couple of times but never made a sound while the two ladies worked. By the time they were done, Ada had stopped crying, but Anthony noticed she seemed lifeless. Her eyes, though dry, had an empty look about them. He wanted so badly to go and repay those girls each with a slap their fathers would feel.

Once the women were done, Ellen turned her attention to Anthony. "Go have Lord Claridge's coach brought around to the side of the house. Then bring him here with her cloak. They can leave through the back exit," she said.

Anthony nodded his head, casting one last look towards Ada before leaving the room. A few minutes later, he returned with Thomas, who appeared visibly agitated. He held Ada's cloak tightly between his hands. Upon seeing his daughter, Thomas crossed the room and gathering her in his arms, letting her cloak fall to the ground beside them. Ada allowed herself to be held, but did not move or raise her arms.

"Let's get you home," Thomas said. Ellen picked up the cloak and handed it back to him. Wrapping it around Ada, Thomas carefully raised the hood up to cover her face.

"Who did this?" Thomas asked, looking at Ellen. His voice was calm, but his eyes betrayed his anger.

"I will find out posthaste," Ellen answered grimly. "Would it be all right to come by tomorrow and check on her?" she asked.

"Yes. I would appreciate that," said Thomas as he held Ada's hand. With a nod of thanks to both Ellen and Eleanor, he allowed Anthony to lead himself and Ada out to their waiting coach.

Ellen and Eleanor returned to the ball, doing their best to appear as if nothing had happened. A few minutes later, Anthony found them, having seen to it Thomas and Ada's carriage left unnoticed.

"Do you know who did that to her?" Ellen asked Anthony. She had a good idea who the culprits might be, but needed confirmation.

"Yes," Anthony responded. Looking around the room, he spotted the girls Ada had been with. They were laughing and chatting with some gentlemen on the other side of the room.

"The girl in the lavender dress, pink dress, and that god-awful purple dress." Anthony said. He knew their names because their mothers had each tried to call his attention to them; now he refused to give them respect.

Eleanor had to bite her lip to keep from laughing at his description. Yes, that color did not compliment Charlotte's complexion, but she wondered if it was the dress or the girl he did not like. Anthony had confirmed her suspicion. Ellen knew them well, for they were the daughters of some high-ranking families.

"Eleanor, please warn Hannah to be careful. If I may ask, would you also inform Lady Ann to keep Dinah away from Charlotte, Penelope, and Rose. But please don't say anything about Ada getting hurt this evening." Ellen looked at her friend, knowing she could be trusted.

"Don't worry. I won't. I know Ada has done some awful things, but seeing her like that, my heart went out to her," answered Eleanor.

"I know. She seemed broken," said Ellen.

Anthony agreed with Ellen. "Everyone makes mistakes, some worse than others, but those girls had no right hurting her like that. They are not innocent," Anthony said. He then turned and walked away.

"He's right about that," Eleanor said as she watched the girls talk and laugh, knowing there would be no repercussions for their actions.

"I don't normally involve Henry in this sort of thing, but I need his advice on handling these girls. Their fathers have business with him," said Ellen.

"Something needs to be done before they do something even worse," Eleanor said. Ellen nodded her head in agreement, her eyes still on the three girls across the room.

* * *

On their way home, Ada didn't say a word. Thomas watched her, feeling guilty for convincing her everything would be okay. "I'm sorry," he said, breaking the silence.

Ada looked up at him. "It's not your fault. I deserved it. After everything I have done," she said.

"No, Ada. You have already paid the price for your wrongdoings. What happened tonight was unconscionable. I will not let anyone hurt you like this again," Thomas said.

"I want to go home and go to bed," Ada said with a tired sigh.

They said nothing more until they were home, and then only a simple goodnight as Ada went upstairs to her room. Thomas hoped Ellen would still come by tomorrow to talk with her. *Maybe she can help her*, he thought, wanting it to be true.

* * *

Anthony was talking with some of the lingering guests at the ball when he noticed his late wife's parents walking toward him. He quickly excused himself, and moved forward to greet them. He loved his in-laws dearly, but it brought up a lot of pain when he was around them.

"Hello, son," Nigel said as they shook hands.

"How have you been?" Anthony asked.

"We have been doing well," Eloise said as she hugged him.

"How about we take a walk?" Nigel suggested.

Once outside on the terrace, Anthony closed his eyes and breathed in deeply, enjoying the cool night air.

"What did you want to talk about?" he asked, opening his eyes, and turning his attention back to the older couple.

"Why haven't you remarried?" Nigel asked bluntly.

Surprised at the question, Anthony did not know how to respond. Nigel and Eloise watched the emotions flit across Anthony's face, seeing his shock give way to sorrow.

"Son, it has been three years. We think it would be best if you started thinking about your future. Genevieve would not want you to be alone for the rest of your life," said Nigel.

"I can't seem to get past the pain," Anthony said as he looked up at the sky, trying to keep from breaking down as he thought of his dead wife.

"I know you loved my daughter, and she loved you. But you have to start thinking about your responsibilities," said Nigel.

"I haven't been ignoring my responsibilities," Anthony replied, surprised that they thought he wasn't taking care of business.

"We know that. What we are referring to is an heir. We don't mean to meddle in your affairs, but we hope you consider your family's future. What will happen to your title and all the people in your employment? All the tenants at your estate? Anthony, you don't have to marry for love, but you must at least try for an heir," said Eloise.

"I know. I promise I will think about it," Anthony said, giving them a weak smile.

"No matter what happens, you will always be our son," Nigel said, embracing Anthony briefly.

"I value your advice, and I know I need to start thinking of the future, but it is difficult. The women I come across have no idea what it feels like to lose something more precious than your own life. Their thoughts are preoccupied with gaining status, and the latest fashion. It's beyond tedious," said Anthony.

"We realize it may be trying, but try to keep an open mind. Someone will come along who will understand you," Eloise said. She hugged him tightly and kissed his cheek lightly.

In that instant, Ada's face popped into Anthony's head. Ada was someone who understood what it is like to lose everything.

Chapter Two

Veronica Aldridge entered her parents' home, finding them having breakfast. "Good morning," she said as she walked to the buffet and selected a plate.

"Well, hello. What do we owe for this surprise visit?" Henry asked as he put down his newspaper.

"I missed my parents and wanted to visit my adorable little stepbrother, Lucien," she said. She artfully balanced her plate, now laden with fresh fruit, hard boiled eggs, and toast, as she maneuvered her way to the table. Her protruding belly made it difficult to eat without dropping food on herself. Once seated, she picked up a piece of toast and carefully began to nibble, occasionally looking down to ensure she had not gotten any crumbs on her dress.

"How's my grandbaby doing?" Henry asked, smiling as he watched his daughter eat.

"Very active lately," Veronica said, setting down the toast and placing a hand on her belly.

"You think it's a girl?" Ellen asked.

"I don't know. I am trying to imagine both," Veronica said, glancing at her stomach with a half-smile. "How was the ball last night?" She asked. Ellen looked down at her plate. "What happened?" Veronica asked immediately.

"There was an incident with a girl," Ellen said, reaching for her teacup and taking a delicate sip.

"Who?" Veronica pressed.

"Ada," Ellen answered. She told Veronica everything that had transpired.

"I hate to hear that happened to her," said Veronica, giving a nod of thanks as a servant set a cup of aromatic herbal tea in front of her.

"Why do you feel pity for her after everything she did?" Henry asked, exasperated.

"Father, she has lost her mother and her reputation. I don't believe she should be punished for the rest of her life. How will she learn to be an upstanding, decent person if nobody gives her a chance," answered Veronica.

Henry was quiet as he mulled over her words. "You are right. Ada should be given a chance," he said finally. Turning towards Ellen, he added, "I will talk to the fathers of the girls responsible for the attack today at the club."

"Who was it that hurt her?" Veronica asked.

"Charlotte, Penelope, and Rose," Ellen answered. Veronica looked down, her face sad. "What is it? Did you have any conflict with them?" Ellen asked.

"Charlotte always treated me terribly. She was often the instigator when they ridiculed me," Veronica said, focusing on the gold detailing of her teacup to avoid looking up. She did not like thinking about the first year she came out into society.

Henry's blood boiled just thinking about those detestable girls hurting his daughter, but he remained calm so as not to upset her in her delicate condition.

"I'm afraid I must depart," he said as he stood and leaned over, giving Ellen a light kiss on the cheek. He then walked over to Veronica and kissed her forehead.

"I love you and my grandchild," he said tenderly, before leaving the room. Heading for the door, his thoughts turned dark. Heads would roll when he confronted the fathers of those horrible girls.

"I made him mad, didn't I?" Veronica asked.

"He is mad, but his anger is not at you," said Ellen grimly. "There must be consequences for what those girls have done. I do wish you had told me when they were hurting you. Perhaps I could have done something to stop it," she said.

"I didn't want to cause trouble for you or father. I thought they would eventually ignore me. Unfortunately, it seems Charlotte and Penelope enjoy hurting people," Veronica said.

"What about Rose?" Ellen asked.

"She never said anything cruel to me. I believe she is caught in a terrible conundrum and cannot escape them," said Veronica.

"And that is precisely why your father needs to stop them before someone gets seriously hurt. I am going to see Ada this morning. I don't think she is handling what happened very well," Ellen said.

"I want to go with you, but I think seeing me right now might cause her additional stress," said Veronica.

"You are probably right. I must go ready myself for the visit," she said as she got up. She walked over to Veronica and kissed her forehead. "Lucien is in his room. Be careful going up and down the stairs," she said before leaving the room.

Veronica no longer felt hungry. Pushing her plate away, she contemplated what she'd learned. She prayed for someone to come into Ada's life. Someone who might change her situation for the better.

* * *

When Ellen arrived at the Claridge home, she was shown the dayroom where Thomas sat reading the newspaper.

"Good morning, Ellen," he said, setting the paper down and getting to his feet. He bowed his head politely. Ellen smiled at his formality, nodding her head in response. Turning to his butler, Thomas said, "Wilkens would you inform Ada I wish to see her." He turned his attention back to Ellen and motioned to the sofa. "Please, have a seat," he said.

"How was Ada last night after you left?" Ellen asked.

"She was very quiet. I am worried about her," Thomas answered truthfully.

"It bothered me how lost she looked. What those girls did to her was horrible. Henry has gone to talk with their fathers," said Ellen.

"I appreciate him defending her, but I am the one who should be doing that," Thomas said.

"We found out this morning those girls also tormented Veronica in the past. So, you can imagine Henry's mood when he left."

"I can't help but feel sorry for those men, thinking what will happen when Henry gets ahold of them," Thomas chuckled. He turned at the sound of the door opening.

Ada entered the room, surprised to see Ellen seated on the sofa across from her father. She lowered her head, hoping to hide her face from the other woman's gaze.

Ellen could tell Ada's eyes were swollen from crying. Acting with motherly instinct, she quickly stood up and went to her, wrapping her arms around her.

Unprepared for Ellen's embrace, Ada initially stiffened, but slowly relaxed. After a moment she wrapped her arms around Ellen and began crying.

Thinking it best to give the ladies some time alone, Thomas quietly stood and left the room. It pained his heart to see his little girl so sad, but he knew Ellen would give his daughter the comfort only a mother could provide.

After Ada stopped crying, she allowed Ellen to guide her over to the sofa and sit her down. "I'm so sorry, I'm afraid I am not myself today," Ada said, attempting a smile.

"That's completely understandable," Ellen said gently. "Sometimes it helps to be able to confide in someone. I'm here for you, dear, if you want to share what's on your mind." Ellen waited patiently, allowing Ada time to collect her thoughts.

Ada looked at Ellen, and felt a tug of grief. She knew she could trust this woman sitting beside her. Ada ached for her own mother, yet simultaneously knew what she longed for was impossible. Taking a deep breath, she began to open up about how things had been since her mother was exiled. Ellen proved to be a patient and understanding listener, which made Ada feel comfortable.

"I know my mother loved me in her own way. But she could not change her nature, and she viewed me as a tool she could wield to further her station in society. She was never satisfied with what she had. I guess I thought if I pleased her, she would at least be satisfied with me."

Ada then told Ellen about what her mother taught her, admitting that her mother had directed her every move. "I know I could have chosen not to do all the horrible things I did. I could have chosen to be kind and selfless—like Veronica. If I had only chosen a different path, none of this would have happened. Instead, I did as my mother asked, allowing myself to be her puppet. And now we both must pay the price," Ada said. "I deserve everything that's happened to me," she added bitterly.

"Nobody deserves to be hurt the way you've been hurt," Ellen said firmly. "You've made some mistakes, but you were only acting as you were taught. Now you know better. You've learned your lesson, and I think a little forgiveness is in order," she said.

"I don't think people are ever going to forgive me," responded Ada.

"I'm not talking about other people's forgiveness. That can be earned, in time. What I mean is that perhaps it's time to forgive yourself for the past and focus on the future," she said.

Ada didn't respond for a while, but looked at Ellen thoughtfully. When she finally spoke, she sounded hopeful. "You've given me much to consider. I am grateful for your visit today. It was so kind and generous of you to come."

"The pleasure is mine, my dear. I am pleased to see you looking a little better," Ellen said. Indeed, Ada did seem to be slightly more animated. Though she still appeared somewhat drawn, there was color in her cheeks once more.

When Ellen finally left, she had a new view of Ada and why she had acted the way she did. The best thing that could have happened to Ada was being away from her mother.

* * *

A few days after the ball, Anthony walked into his parents' home, ready for a fight. He had come to a decision about something, and he knew they would not be happy. Mathew and Ruth Carlyle were in the dayroom waiting for their son, having received a letter only hours earlier that stated he needed a meeting. Anthony and his father had never been close, their communication always feeling more like business transactions, but he loved his mother dearly. As a child it was she who would console him, always showing him the love and support a boy needed. As he walked into the room, his mother stood and walked to him, hugging him. Reflexively, he put his arms around her and hugged her back.

"Why did you want to see us?" Mathew asked, wasting no time on pleasantries.

"I had the opportunity to speak with Genevieve's parents at the ball. They feel I have grieved long enough and it's time to move on. Upon reflection of their words, I have decided to remarry," Anthony responded simply. He dropped his arms and took a step back from his mother.

Silence filled the room as his parents digested the news. Finally, Ruth smiled wide and hugged him again. "I am so happy to think I will be gaining another daughter-in-law and that I will eventually have grandchildren to love!" She said. Suddenly, her smile faded and she looked stricken. Letting him go, she said, "I'm so sorry, Anthony! I didn't mean to sound so heartless. You know I loved Genevieve."

"I know, mother. It's okay," Anthony said, smiling at her.

"So, who is the girl?" Mathew asked.

"I need you both to sit down and listen to what I have to say," Anthony said.

When Mathew and Ruth had settled themselves on the sofa, Anthony took a seat in one of the mahogany wood chairs situated directly across from them.

"I had no plans to remarry because I didn't think I would find someone who could understand what it felt like to lose something that meant everything to them."

"And now you have?" Ruth asked gently.

"Yes. But I have yet to speak to her father. I wanted to inform both of you first, so you would be prepared for the gossip."

"Who is it?" Mathew asked, frowning.

"Lord Claridge, the Earl of Kingsley's daughter," Anthony said. He sat back, waiting for the inevitable rant from his father. Ruth was stunned into silence.

"Who is she?" Mathew asked, looking at his wife.

"Ada," said Ruth in a low voice.

"Do you mean the girl rumored to have had relations with Malcolm Randolph, whose parents divorced, and whose mother was forced to leave town?" Mathew asked in a raised, disbelieving voice.

"Yes," replied Anthony. He looked his father in the eye, showing him he was serious.

"No, you will not marry her. You would bring shame into this house and upon our name," yelled Mathew as he rose to his feet and began pacing.

"Mother, do you have something to say?" Anthony asked, turning his attention away from his father.

Ruth looked up at Anthony sadly and stared at him for a long moment before letting out a long breath. "Why her? Yes, she has lost her mother and her reputation. But other girls have lost things also. Surely she must not be the only one who could appreciate what you've been through," she said.

"The girl was attacked at the ball by some of the daughters of "higher station," Anthony said, using sarcasm at the end of this statement to convey his disgust that these young women might be considered more deserving of respect. "I saw something in Ada I hadn't seen in others. The only way I can describe it is that she appeared to be completely shattered. Like her spirit had been broken and she'd lost all hope. As strange as it may sound, I could relate to that," he said in a subdued voice.

"Oh that poor dear," Ruth said, unconsciously lifting one hand to her throat. She was a soft-hearted person who never gossiped, never causing anyone to feel uncomfortable.

"I don't care what happened to her. That girl is not an appropriate marital candidate for a member of this family," Mathew said in a calm, firm voice, as if he assumed Anthony would obey his words.

"She is still the daughter of an earl. An earl who is best friends with Lord Aldridge," Anthony said, knowing his father cared deeply about rubbing elbows with the upper peerage. He could tell his words had hit their intended mark, and that his father was already considering the potential advantage of Lord Claridge as Anthony's father-in-law. Anthony had never let his father know that he already had business dealings with Ellis and Henry Aldridge. He knew his father would have demanded to be involved, which was the last thing Anthony wanted.

Ruth had to look away as she tried to contain her smile. She knew Anthony was manipulating her husband and wouldn't attempt to stop him. It had always bothered her that her husband put wealth and status above his family.

"How would you handle the backlash from marrying her?" Mathew asked speculatively.

"The first thing I would do is talk to her father and get his approval. I enlisted Lady Aldridge's help last night to take care of Ada. I can also ask her to help deal with the ton when news of our engagement becomes public. She would have no problem assisting me in this matter," Anthony said confidently.

Anthony knew his father's mind was working, and that he was thinking of how he might use the esteem Henry and his wife had for Anthony to his advantage. It made Anthony sick to watch his father drool over the idea of keeping company with the Marquess. He already had to keep a tight leash on his father after he had almost ruined their family, spending their fortune trying to live above his means. It had taken Anthony several years, and had involved some unethical actions that would remain a secret, to keep them off the street.

"Mother, what do you think?" Anthony asked, turning his attention once again to Ruth.

"I don't know her personally, but I knew her mother. Agnes was an awful person. She took pleasure in the downfall of others. I feared her daughter would be like her, but if Lady Ellen is willing to help, she must see some good in her."

"Ada will not anticipate my proposal, though she'll no doubt be grateful for it. I expect she'll be a compliant wife," Anthony said.

Ruth looked affronted by his arrogance. "I won't allow you to be cruel to her. She might be ruined in the eyes of polite society, but that doesn't give anybody the right to take advantage of her," she said with a sniff.

"Mother, I would never raise my hand to any woman," Anthony said, surprised she would think that of him. "I only meant that I think she will not revert to old behaviors, but will remain amenable because she will appreciate the social benefit that marriage to me will afford her.

"Even so, there are so many ways to hurt someone. Ignoring them, and acting like they don't matter can hurt even more than a fist," Ruth said, looking down. Anthony knew she was referring to herself and that his father had never been a good, attentive husband.

"I might never love her, but I would never treat her dismissively, or uncaringly," Anthony said.

Ruth was quiet for a moment watching her son. "If this is what you want, I won't stop you," she said.

"What say you, father?" Anthony asked.

"I also won't stand in your way as long as the union doesn't hurt your social standing," said Mathew, rejoining his wife on the sofa.

"Then I must take my leave. I have sent a message to Lord Claridge requesting an audience and I am awaiting his reply," said Anthony. He stood and walked over to his mother, then kissed her on the head. His father stood, and the two men shook hands.

Moments later, Anthony was sitting in his carriage, on his way home. He could not stop himself from smiling. His father was so predictable. All he'd done was mentioned the Aldridge name, and his father had acted like a dog chasing a ball.

* * *

Thomas was in his office when he received Anthony's note. *Anthony Carlyle? Why does he want to see me?* He thought, puzzled. Thinking back to that disastrous night at the ball, Thomas wondered if it had something to do with what had happened. He quickly penned a reply, agreeing to meet Anthony that afternoon, then arranged for his note to be delivered.

* * *

A little while later, Ada was walking down the passageway that led to the main hall when she heard a knock sound at the door. *We're not expecting visitors... Perhaps it's someone for Father,* she thought. She paused just out of sight, waiting to learn who was calling before revealing her presence. Her blood ran cold as she recognized the voice of their morning caller. With fear gripping her, she ran to a nearby alcove and hid. Leaning against the wall, she forced herself to breathe again. With her breathing under control, she slowly sank down the wall and wrapped her arms around her body.

"Malcolm Randolph to see Lord Claridge," Ada heard the caller say.

"I will go and inform my lord you are here," replied the butler.

Ada started to shake, as memories of that terrible day came flooding back. The pain and humiliation of what he had done to her became overwhelming, and tears ran down her face. She had told nobody but her mother the truth about what happened that day; now he was in her house.

"This way," said Wilkens leading the caller to her father's office. Ada slowly got up as she heard the door shut, willing her trembling legs to move. Taking a deep breath, she ran to her room, closing and bolting the door behind her. She immediately walked over to her bed, reached under her pillow, and pulled out a knife. Moving to furthest corner of the room, she again sank to the floor, still clutching the knife. She was terrified Malcolm Randolph had come to take her away. That he'd come to hurt her again.

* * *

"Why are you here?" demanded Thomas as he stood up from behind his desk. He didn't bother to disguise his anger that Malcolm was in his home.

"I have come to make an offer of marriage for your lovely daughter," said Malcolm, not waiting for an invitation as he sat down in the chair positioned on the opposite side of the desk.

"You what?" asked Thomas, entirely caught off guard.

"I wish to marry your daughter," He repeated with a smirk.

Stunned by the other man's audacity, Thomas could not keep his voice from rising. "No, hell no! She is ruined because you spread false rumors, and now you dare to walk into my home and expect me to let you marry her?"

Malcolm appeared unperturbed. He flicked an imaginary speck of lint from the breast of his silk waistcoat before responding. "Well, I am not surprised you discovered it was me who started the rumors. But since I was the one behind Ada's fall from grace, I now want to make things right by marrying her."

"Get out of my house," said Thomas as he tried to control his anger. Malcolm stood slowly, unaffected by Thomas's rejection.

"I will not withdraw my offer just yet. I will wait a little longer for you to realize she has no other choice." Malcolm moved closer to Thomas. Leaning forward, he whispered in the older man's ear. "When I want something, I always get it," he said in a voice that left no doubt in Thomas's mind what he meant.

"Walter, please see this... gentleman... to the door," Thomas said in a voice that was now shaking with rage. He knew his butler would be standing just outside the door. Turning his back to the other man, he waited for Walter to usher him out before collapsing heavily into his chair.

Putting his elbows on his desk Thomas buried his face in his hands. *How do I protect my little girl from that monster?* he wondered. *He is the kind of man who takes what he wants. He could forcibly take Ada and disappear...* His head flew up suddenly at the thought. Running out of his office and up the stairs to Ada's room, he knocked soundly on her door. There was no response.

"Ada, are you in there?" He called.

"Father, is that you?" Came Ada's reply.

Thomas pressed his head against the door with relief. "Yes, it's me," he said. He heard her unbolt the door, and took a step back. The door slowly opened as Ada peeked out. Seeing her father, she opened it wide and ran into his arms. Thomas could feel her shaking as he held her.

"Is he gone?" She asked, never raising her head from Thomas's chest.

"Yes, he is gone," Thomas assured her. "At least for now. But Ada, now that we know he's in town, I will need you to stay at the house. You're only to leave if I am with you. Do you understand?" He said in a serious voice.

Ada stepped back and looked at him. "He wants to take me away, doesn't he?" She whispered.

"He wants to marry you. But that is never going to happen," said Thomas. Ada began sobbing as Thomas pulled her back into his arms. "I will protect you at all costs," he said. Thomas let her cry for a while, then separated himself from her and wiped her face with a handkerchief he extracted from his pocket.

Ada took a deep breath to try and calm down.

"I need to go and send word to Henry," said Thomas. Henry despised Malcolm, and knew well how dangerous he was. He would be willing to help Thomas protect his daughter from the man. "I want you to stay in your room today in case he comes back. You can have one of the maids bring you some books and food. Do you understand?" Thomas said.

"Yes, father. I will do as you say," said Ada.

Thomas smiled and kissed Ada's forehead. He watched her as she retreated back into her room, then waited until he heard the bolt of the door slide into place before returning to his office. Once there, he wrote a quick note to tell Henry he needed help, then sat down heavily, wondering how he was going to keep his daughter safe.

* * *

That afternoon, Thomas was still in his office when the butler informed him Lord Carlyle had arrived. Thomas had forgotten all about his meeting with Anthony. "Show him in," he said.

"Good afternoon, Lord Claridge," said Anthony. Thomas stood and shook his hand.

"Lord Carlyle, please sit. How can I assist you?" said Thomas.

"I would like to make an offer of marriage to your daughter," Anthony said once he was seated.

Thomas was speechless. It was the last thing he expected from someone as upstanding as Anthony. "You wish to marry Ada?" Thomas asked.

"Yes," answered Anthony.

"I must admit this is most unexpected. You will have heard the rumors..." Thomas said. It pained him to speak of Ada's tarnished reputation so openly, but he needed to know Anthony understood her situation.

"Yes, I know," Anthony said, unperturbed.

"Well then... why?" Thomas asked, unable to hide his bewilderment.

"I'm sure you're aware that my wife died in childbirth several years ago. I've decided it's time for me to remarry," Anthony said.

"Yes, I'd heard what happened. It was most tragic. But that still doesn't explain why... Ada?" Thomas persisted.

Anthony looked down, wondering if Thomas would understand his reasoning. "I have had several young ladies presented to me—all of whom have made their interest... abundantly clear... but none of them are in possession of substance... of depth. They are immature, preoccupied with status, material wealth, drama, and gossip. None of them know what it is to lose something precious to them."

"And Ada does," Thomas said, more to himself than Anthony.

"Yes. I saw the look in her eyes that night at the ball. In that moment I saw that she, more than anyone, would understand what I felt. I might not love her as I did my wife, but I would never mistreat her or be anything but a good husband," Anthony said earnestly.

Thomas was quiet for a moment, as he contemplated Anthony's words. He wished the events of the morning had not happened. "I would like nothing more than for my daughter to marry a man like you," he began. "But there is something you need to know—" Before Thomas could finish, Walter entered the room again, announcing that Lord Aldridge had arrived.

"Please show him in," Thomas said. When his butler left, he turned to Anthony, "I will explain everything shortly."

Anthony and Thomas both stood as Henry walked in.

"Lord Carlyle," Henry said, surprised to see him.

"Lord Aldridge," replied Anthony, bowing his head.

"Thank you for coming, Henry," said Thomas.

"Your note was quite troubling. What has happened?" Henry asked.

"I received a visit from Randolph," said Thomas.

Henry froze for an instant, wondering why Malcolm would have the nerve to show his face. It was not a good sign. He looked at Anthony, then at Thomas. "Perhaps we should discuss the matter privately?" he suggested.

"Lord Carlyle needs to hear this, since he has just extended an offer of marriage to Ada," Thomas said.

Henry looked at Anthony as they sat down, astonished and relieved in equal measure. "You are a good man, Anthony, and I believe Ada would make a good wife. Although I admit, knowing your father, I am surprised. I cannot see him agreeing to this match," he said.

"It took some persuading, but he did in the end," said Anthony.

"So, what does this have to do with Randolph?" Henry asked.

"He too, wants to marry Ada," Thomas said. The other two men looked taken aback.

"I understand," Henry said finally.

"Understand what?" Thomas asked.

"Randolph does nothing that doesn't benefit him. So, when he set the rumor in motion that ruined Ada, I couldn't understand what he had to gain," Henry began.

"You think the only way he could get a member of the peerage to allow him to marry their daughter was to leave no other option," said Anthony with dawning awareness.

"Yes, my guess is that was his plan. None of the gentlemen I know would allow a man like Randolph to come near their daughters. He may have money, but even those who are desperate for funds know it would be social suicide to have their family name tied to Randolph. Not to mention, no one with even the slightest affection for their child would allow them near that man. Certainly not after what he did to his last mistress at White's Gentlemen's Club," Henry said grimly.

"Are you referring to the time he dragged a woman out into the halls in nothing but her shift, then beat her?" Anthony asked with disgust.

"Yes," replied Henry.

"Why now, and why Ada?" Thomas asked.

"She is your only child. And your brother..." Henry began.

"Has only daughters," said Thomas, nodding.

"If Ada were to have a boy—" continued Henry.

"I would leave everything to my grandson," Thomas finished.

"And a year or two after your grandson's birth, you would then have an unexpected accident. That would leave Randolph in charge until the boy comes of age, giving him exactly what he wants," Anthony said.

"Yes. A bloody brilliant plan," Henry said, causing Thomas and Anthony to look at him. "Oh, you have to admit it is a brilliant plan. Evil, but brilliant," he said. He looked between the other two men, causing Thomas to chuckle.

"So, how do we stop him?" Thomas asked.

"Our good man here," said Henry, patting Anthony on the shoulder, "has already blown his plan right out of the water."

Anthony and Thomas looked at each other, then at Henry, waiting for him to tell them how.

"Because Anthony wants to marry Ada," said Henry, holding up his hands as if they should already know this. "You know the first thing he will do now?" He said, looking at Anthony.

"He will come to talk to me. Try to get me to change my mind," said Anthony.

"And when that doesn't work?" Thomas asked.

"He will go to your father. Thinking he can force you to call things off," said Henry.

"Randolph doesn't know that my father looks down on people who are lower in standing than him. So he might not even give Randolph an audience if he tries to come to his home."

"Even so, Anthony, it could be dangerous dealing with a man like him. If you choose to cry off, I will completely understand," Thomas said. Although Thomas wanted what was best for his daughter, he knew what Malcolm Randolph was capable of. Marrying Ada was not worth risking Anthony's life.

Anthony looked at Thomas and smiled. "I will never cower or run from a man like Malcolm Randolph. So, I stand behind my offer for Ada," he said.

Henry reached over to grab Anthony's shoulder. "I always knew you were an honest, stand up man," he said.

"I would be proud for my daughter to marry a man like you, but I can't help but worry." Thomas said. He took a deep breath and looked at Henry, who nodded his head yes. "All right, I accept your offer," he said turning to Anthony.

"Do you think we should inquire as to what Ada thinks?" Anthony asked with a teasing smile.

"Oh, he will make an excellent husband," Henry said, chuckling.

"I will speak with her this afternoon once she's had some time to settle down," said Thomas.

"What's wrong?" Anthony asked.

"She knew Randolph was here. I've never seen her so scared. She asked me if he was here to take her away. I've asked her to remain in her room for the time being, in case Randolph returns and attempts something foolish. But I will need both of you to help me keep her safe. Although Ada's reputation has been compromised, the engagement must be done appropriately so there will be no gossip to hurt your family. As well, the engagement will mean Ada will be back out in society again, which means she will be vulnerable."

"I agree. We will need to have a chaperone with us at all times when we are out. And we will always be on guard," said Anthony.

"I am sending one of my private guards, Aaron, to you to be Ada's shadow. I have trusted him to protect Ellen and Veronica for years. You will rarely see him, but he will always be with her," Henry said.

"I appreciate the offer, but don't you still need him?" asked Thomas.

"I still have William, and we are staying with Veronica. She is due any day now and won't be going anywhere." Henry couldn't help but smile at the thought of becoming a grandfather for the second time.

"Soon to be a grandfather," Thomas said, smiling.

"Congratulations," Anthony said.

"Thank you. I could not be happier," said Henry, beaming. He stood, causing Anthony and Thomas to get to their feet as well. "The sooner I get home, the sooner I can send Ada some protection," he said.

"I can't tell you what it means to me to have your friendship. I don't know what I would do without you," said Thomas as he moved to escort his friend across the room to the door.

"We have been friends most of our lives. I will never leave a friend when things get dangerous. You know how much I like a good fight," Henry said.

"Yes, I do," Thomas said, chuckling.

"Anthony, I will be seeing you soon," said Henry as he left the room.

"I should be going myself. I will send a letter formally stating my intent to visit tomorrow morning. If that is all right with you?" Anthony said as he walked up to Thomas and shook his hand.

"Yes, please do have lunch with us tomorrow. I did not think it possible for someone as worthy as you to express interest in my daughter after what happened. For her sake, I am most grateful. However, I do want you to be careful. Randolph will be angry once he knows of your intention to marry Ada."

"I will be diligent at all times, and especially when Ada is in my care. I will keep her safe," Anthony promised before he too, left the room.

Thomas stood there for a few minutes, reviewing everything that had happened. He decided he needed to go ahead and tell Ada about Anthony. She would need time to adjust to the idea of their betrothal, and prepare for courtship. Walking upstairs to her room, he knocked on her door softly. "Ada, it's me," he said.

Ada opened the door, and Thomas stepped inside. "Has something else happened?" she asked.

"So much has happened since this morning." Thomas said, smiling. He pulled her in for a hug.

"Father, what's going on?" she asked.

"I need you to come over here and sit down," Thomas said as he held her hand, guiding her over to sit by the fire. "I had a visitor a little while ago. It seems things are about to change for you," he said.

Ada looked at her father, not sure what was happening. "Who came to visit?" She asked.

"Lord Anthony Carlyle. He came to ask permission to court you," he said.

"He did what?" She asked.

"He wants to marry you," said Thomas. Ada was speechless. "You have met him, haven't you?" he asked.

"I have seen him, but I haven't officially met him. Why would he want to marry me?" She asked. Ada remembered seeing him once at a ball, but not since then. She thought she might have seen him at his family's ball the night Charlotte and the others attacked her. *Had it been him in the room that night?* She wondered. She couldn't remember.

"He needs to marry for an heir. I know you have probably heard people talk about his late wife," Thomas said.

"I remember hearing something about her, but I'm afraid I don't know all the details," Ada said.

"She died in childbirth, and so did his child," said Thomas.

"Oh, that's awful," said Ada, raising a hand to her mouth in shock.

"Yes, it is. Sometimes people have a hard time getting over tragedy like that. He wants someone who understands him. You have suffered in a way most could never imagine, which means you can relate to his pain. He needs someone like that in his life."

Ada looked at the fire, in deep thought. So many emotions were flowing through her. She wanted to feel pleased, but she had so many reservations. Anthony seemed like an upstanding gentleman who would not take part in cruel games. He would not have approached her father unless he was serious. *But even so, why me?* She wondered. "If he were to marry someone like Charlotte Smitherman, she would have no idea how to understand him. So, I understand why he wouldn't want that, but won't his family disapprove of me?" She asked.

"He said they have no objection," her father answered.

"Could I truly marry a man like Viscount Carlyle?" She asked, still not quite believing it was true.

"Yes, I have already agreed, and he will call on you tomorrow." He saw her smile for the first time in a while, and hated having to ruin it. "Ada, I need you to be very careful if you go out in public with him. Randolph will be angry and he will probably do something atrocious in response to the news of your betrothal to Anthony. So, I want you to be careful about your surroundings and be aware of who is around you."

"Father, what if he does something to Lord Carlyle? That man is truly evil," she said.

Thomas could visibly see the hope in her eyes being replaced by dread. "Anthony is aware of the dangers and will take appropriate precautions," he said. "Henry is sending one of his guards here to protect you. You might not see him, but rest assured he will be watching and protecting you."

"Truly?" Ada asked.

"Yes, but you must act normal and not draw attention to yourself. It might not be very comfortable for a while, but eventually, things will improve. I don't want you worrying about anything except your betrothal to Lord Carlyle. He is your priority now. Let him see the goodness within you, so that he may learn to admire you, and perhaps one day care for you as I do. Do you understand?"

"Yes, father," she said as they stood and hugged.

"Be brave, sweetheart. Everything will be okay," Thomas said. He kissed her forehead, then left her room.

Ada stood there thinking about Lord Carlyle—his tall, broad shoulders, his reddish-brown wavy hair, and his beautiful dark blue eyes. It was clear he took excellent care of himself, which only added to his good looks. Ada wondered if it was a dream, that a man as handsome and respectable as Lord Carlyle would want to marry her. But fear gripped her heart as she thought about the possibility of Malcolm Randolph coming between them. In her heart, she knew that was precisely what would happen.

Chapter Three

The following day, Anthony arrived at the Claridge home. For some reason, he felt a little anxious about seeing Ada. He hoped she would be receptive to him and the idea of marriage. He knew how it felt to close off your heart, and even though he would never love her, he would do his best to be a good husband. He missed having someone to come home to and talk to when he had a trying day. He hoped Ada wasn't one of those brainless chits whose only interest was shopping. He started wondering if he should have talked to her before offering marriage. *Well, too late to think of that now you fool*, he silently admonished himself.

* * *

Ada sat in front of the mirror while her maid finished pinning her hair. Lucy was an older woman who had worked in the Claridge home for several years.

"You look lovely," said Lucy.

"Thank you," Ada replied.

Lucy froze, not used to Ada being polite. Noticing the look on Lucy's face, Ada turned to around. "I'm sorry for how I used to be towards you. You were always so good at taking care of me, and I treated you horribly," she said.

"It's okay, miss," said Lucy, smiling.

"No, it's not. I was horrible, and I want you to know I am sorry," Ada said.

"Things are looking up for you, miss. You deserve something good." Lucy said earnestly.

"Thank you, Lucy. I am so nervous. What if he decides he doesn't like me?" Said Ada.

"Just be yourself. You are a bright, intelligent girl. A gentleman like Lord Carlyle would value a lady who can hold her own in a conversation," said Lucy.

"You know of Lord Carlyle?" This surprised Ada.

"I worked for his first wife's parents before she was married. God rest her soul," said Lucy as she made the sign of the cross. "She was a lot like you... very beautiful," she said.

"She was beautiful?" Asked Ada. It had not occurred to her previously to wonder what Anthony's wife had been like, but now she desperately wanted to know.

"Yes, very beautiful. She was tall and slender, with light blonde hair and big green eyes," answered Lucy.

"Completely different from me then," said Ada looking down. How could he want her when she looked nothing like the woman he loved?

"Oh, miss, that's a good thing," said Lucy, seeing it bothered Ada.

"It is?" Ada asked.

"Yes, He will see you for you and not a ghost of his past. So, you have a chance to make a new beginning with him," said Lucy.

Ada thought about what Lucy's words, and decided she was right. This was a chance for both of them to start fresh. Ada rose and stepped closer to Lucy so that the two women were face to face. Lucy smiled, unsure what to do. Without warning, Ada reached out to embrace her servant. Lucy let out a squeak of surprise, then hugged her back warmly.

"Miss Ada, I want you to go down there and show Lord Carlyle what a wonderful young woman you are," Lucy said. She stepped back and straightened the lace that trimmed the collar of Ada's dress, then nodded her approval.

Ada walked to the door and reached for the handle then paused. Taking a deep breath, she straightened her shoulders, opened the door, and exited the room.

Anthony was just walking through the front entrance as Ada came down the stairs. Looking up, he saw her and had to admit she was beautiful. Her long chestnut brown hair was pulled back and tied with a ribbon, revealing her long slender neck. She wore a peach gown with long sleeves and lace around the collar. It was pretty but modest, which surprised him. Most girls dressed far more seductively, in hopes of catching his attention. Ada's choice of apparel demonstrated she still had some self-respect, which pleased him immensely. She smiled as she approached him, but he could tell she was nervous.

"Lord Carlyle, welcome," she said as she curtsied.

"Please, call me Anthony. I look forward to getting to know you," he said, kissing her hand briefly.

Ada couldn't help but blush a little, which flustered her. She had always been confident, and never had any man made her blush. Thomas appeared in that moment, having just come out of his office. Ada was grateful for the distraction as it gave her time to recover her composure.

"Anthony, perfect timing," said Thomas. The two men shook hands warmly. "Let's eat. Ada, you look lovely," he added. He took Ada's hand and kissed it.

"Thank you, father," said Ada as the trio made their way into the dining room.

Thomas sat with Anthony to his left and Ada to his right. Initially, the conversation was mainly between the men, but as the meal progressed

Anthony began to ask what Ada thought about various current events. Each time, Ada gave him her honest opinion, which pleased him. She was well-informed and had good points, and this made him smile. He was glad he could hold an intelligent conversation with her.

"Why don't you go into the drawing room and talk some more?" Thomas suggested as they rose from the table at the end of the meal. "Just leave the door open, and I'll have Wilkens stand at the door for proprieties sake," he added.

"Would you like to sit with me for a bit longer?" Ada asked shyly.

"Yes, I would," Anthony replied with a smile.

His smile is infectious, Ada thought, feeling the corners of her own mouth lift in response. However, once they were seated, and the maid had left after bringing tea, things became awkward. Ada was silent, waiting for Anthony to speak first.

"Ada, we need to talk about some things to move forward. Is that all right with you?" he finally said.

"Yes, it is," answered Ada. "I wish to be open and honest with you," she said. She reached for the teapot and poured him a steaming cup, then started pouring one for herself.

"I know about Randolph wanting to marry you—" Anthony began. Ada's hand began to shake, causing her to spill some of the hot liquid on her hand. Anthony quickly reached for a hand towel as she set her cup down. Taking her hand, he gently dabbed it, noticing her whole body was shaking.

"I'm sorry. I am not normally so clumsy," she said, giving Anthony a slight smile.

Anthony knew something was gravely wrong by her reaction at the mere mention of Randolph's name. He could see genuine fear in her eyes, and realized there must be more to the story than her father and Henry knew.

"Why are you so afraid of him?" he asked quietly.

Ada opened her mouth to say something but closed it again and looked down.

"You can tell me anything. I promise I will not judge you. But I need to know the truth because he will undoubtedly come to me to stop our engagement. If I know your history beforehand, there will be nothing he can do or say to cause any trouble," Anthony said.

Ada looked up at him, unable to stop the tears from forming in her eyes. She knew she needed to tell him the truth so she took a deep, calming breath, then let it out slowly. "I wasn't with him voluntarily," she whispered, closing her eyes. She didn't notice the tears streaming down her face.

Without any thought of propriety, Anthony instinctively pulled her into his arms and held her close as she cried. What she said didn't surprise him because of the way she had reacted with so much fear. He had seen it before in other women who had been accosted.

After a few minutes, Ada sat up straight. Anthony handed her a handkerchief to wipe her face. Instead, she used it to brush the dampness of her tears from his waistcoat.

"I'm sorry I messed up your clothes," she said apologetically.

He smiled at her as she studied the offending spot, futilely trying to erase the evidence of her sadness.

"It's okay. I think it will dry," he said smiling.

Gently taking the handkerchief from her, he lifted it to her face. She froze as he leaned closer to her and softly wiped the moisture from her cheeks.

"Why haven't you told anyone about what happened?" he asked in a low voice, trying not to upset her again.

"I told no one but my mother," she answered.

Anthony noticed the faraway look in Ada's eyes. "Your father doesn't know?" He said, surprised.

"No, father never asked for details when the rumors started," Ada answered.

"How did you come across... him?" Anthony asked. He was careful not to say Malcolm's name. In his experience, sometimes minor details like that helped make it easier to open up.

"My mother sent me to ask him for help. I don't know how she knew him. She wouldn't say," said Ada.

Anthony was shocked that a mother would send her daughter to see a monster like Randolph. "Why did you need his help?" He asked.

Ada looked away, not wanting to tell him that her mother had planned to take Veronica's money and ruin her. She was afraid of seeing the disgust she felt for herself reflected on his face.

"Ada?" he asked.

She didn't look at him as she told him how she had taken part in her mother's plan to force Owen Pierce to marry Veronica. She spared none of the details, telling him of their plan to compromise Veronica so Owen would have reason to divorce her and then marry Ada. Anthony was speechless—not because he didn't believe someone could be that cruel, but at the thought of a mother enlisting their daughter in such a despicable act.

"I have learned much from Veronica since all this happened," Ada said.

"How so?" Anthony asked.

"After everything we did and planned to do, Veronica has shown me nothing but kindness and understanding. She never shunned me when my parents divorced, nor when the rumors surfaced and my reputation came into question. My mother taught me that compassion was a weakness and that people would take advantage of you if you were kind to them. She said I must always show strength and keep others in their place," Ada said. She paused, choosing her next words with care.

"But Veronica has shown me differently. Compassion is not weakness, and helping instead of hurting is the right way to act," she said.

Anthony thought that Ada's mother would have been a good match for his own father. They had the same kind of arrogance. He was impressed that Ada could see the error in her mother's teachings. "You are wise to have learned to change your ways and become a better person," he said.

Ada looked up at him, surprised. "I was afraid you would be disgusted by me after hearing how horrible I was," she said.

"Hearing you admit your mistakes and making strides to change tells me all I need to know about you," Anthony answered. He could see her physically relax upon hearing his words. Although he hated to bring it back up and cause her more pain, he still needed to know what had happened between her and Randolph. "Ada, I really need you to tell me everything," he said.

Ada looked at him, then looked at the door, silently signaling that someone was standing right outside.

Understanding her unspoken concern, Anthony stood up, offering Ada his arm. Ada stood automatically, accepting it gracefully but looking a little puzzled.

"I thought perhaps we might go for a stroll out of doors," he suggested.

"That would be delightful," Ada answered, her expression clearing.

As they left the room, Ada turned to Walter. "Would you please ask Lucy to accompany us out into the courtyard," she asked.

While they waited for Lucy, Anthony lifted the hand Ada was using to hold his arm and clasped it in his own. The act was sweet and loving, and it made Ada feel more secure. At the sound of Lucy's footsteps, Anthony gave her hand one last, comforting squeeze and then let go, resuming his air of formality. The two walked through the courtyard to the garden, where they seated themselves upon a bench. Lucy stayed a short distance away, to give them a little privacy.

Turning towards Ada, Anthony took her hand again, this time putting it between both of his. "I know this is difficult, but I must know the details about what happened," he said, looking into her eyes. Ada nodded slowly.

"As I said, my mother told me to contact him about helping to compromise Veronica," she began. "He told me to meet him at the gentlemen's club. When I arrived at the side door, a young boy was waiting. He took me to a room where Malcolm was waiting. We discussed what my mother wanted him to do, and he agreed to help on one condition. I told him I could pay him a large sum... but he said it wasn't money he wanted." Ada paused, lost in her memories. "He said he wanted me to... service him in bed. I said no, I wasn't here for that. I turned to leave, but he grabbed me and threw me against the wall. He put his hand around my throat, and I couldn't breathe," she said. Ada raised her hand to her throat as she remembered the pain. A fresh wave of tears streamed down her face, but she remained calm. "I tried to stop him, but he was so strong. I looked to the boy standing by the door for help, but he just stood there with his eyes downcast. I thought I would die. Eventually, I passed out." Ada stopped talking.

Anthony noticed her begin to tremble. He took her other hand, so he could hold the two between his own. He noted how cold hers felt, but said nothing, wanting her to continue.

"When I woke up, he was on top of me. He had raised my skirt and was..." She stopped talking and began sobbing. Gathering her into his arms, Anthony held her again while she cried.

Lucy slowly walked towards them. "Please, forgive me for intruding, but you must tell him the rest. It would be best to show him," Lucy said in a low voice.

"What's she talking about?" Anthony asked. Ada looked down again, and was quiet. "Ada, what is she talking about?" he asked again. Not bothering with his handkerchief this time, he gently raised her chin then brushed her tears away with his hands. Ada looked into his eyes, seeing only concern and sadness.

"When he was finished, he put me on my stomach and held a knife to my throat. He said if I screamed, he would cut my face up and make me ugly," Ada said, then paused, taking another breath. "He cut the back of my dress and the strings to my stays." She stopped talking and stood on shaking legs. Anthony stood with her and grasped her arm, steadying her.

"Lucy, will you help me?" Ada asked as she turned her back to him and unbuttoned the front of her dress. Lucy walked behind her and pulled the dress down just low enough to begin unlacing her stays.

Not too far away from them, Aaron stood watching and listening. He was surprised at what he had heard. He felt a little guilty now about initial reaction upon learning he had been temporarily reassigned and was to come and protect Ada. He had not wanted to, because Ada had once tried to hurt Veronica. Aaron and the other guards had all thought Ada was hateful and disgusting and deserved everything that had happened to her. Now he thought maybe they'd been too quick to judge. He vowed to do everything in his power to protect her.

After a couple of strings were loosened, Lucy pulled the stays open and pulled down Ada's shift right below her shoulder blade. Anthony couldn't help but gasp when he saw the initials MR carved into her back. Ada didn't say anything as Lucy started pulling her strings closed again. Once her dress was properly closed, Ada turned to Anthony, but would not look at him. He did not say anything as he walked to her, and gathered her gently in his arms once more. She did not cry, but wrapped her arms around him and laid her head on his chest. She felt as if a weight had been lifted for the first time since the terrible event had happened.

"I promise you. Nobody will ever hurt you like that again. I don't care what anyone says. We will be married, and you will never have to fear him again," Anthony said.

"I don't deserve someone as good as you, but I'm so thankful to have you," said Ada.

Anthony pulled back and looked at Ada with a gentle smile. "I know this has been difficult for you. Why don't you go to your room now and rest. I want you to relax and let your mind settle itself again. All right?" He said.

Ada smiled at him and nodded. She quickly kissed his cheek, then hurried back inside, with Lucy trailing behind her. His smile fell as he watched her walk away.

"You can come out now," said Anthony, not moving.

Aaron emerged from behind the bushes. "Hello, Captain," he said.

"I haven't been called captain for a long time. It's good to see you again," Anthony said as he turned and shook Aaron's hand. "How long have you worked for Henry?" He asked.

"For several years now. Michael, Ian, and William also work for him. After you left the crown's service, we decided it was time to look for something else," Aaron said. He looked away as old memories of the kind of work he had done as a spy returned. The lives they had to take still haunt him.

"I had heard. Several of our men went to work for me. I am relieved Henry sent you to watch over Ada. We must not let anything happen to her," said Anthony.

"No, sir. I will not let that vile excuse for a man anywhere near her," Aaron said with resolve.

"Yes, he is despicable. I must talk to Thomas now. But I will see you again soon," said Anthony. Aaron nodded, watching Anthony return to the house in search of Thomas.

Anthony felt relieved to know Aaron was guarding Ada. He and Aaron had served together in the royal navy and on other endeavors, and Anthony trusted him completely. Anthony's own home was fully staffed with men from his time in the service. He found he only trusted men he had fought beside—men who had proven their loyalty and ability during times of crisis. When he got back to the house Walter escorted him to Thomas, who was in his office, working.

"Oh, Anthony. Where is Ada?" Thomas asked.

"I sent her to her room to rest. I need to discuss some things with you. Things that she told me," Anthony answered.

"All right, please sit," said Thomas, who was still seated behind his desk. He wondered whether Anthony had changed his mind about Ada.

"I don't know if she wants you to hear what happened with Randolph, but I think you need to know the truth," Anthony said as he sat down.

"The truth?" asked Thomas, confused. He grew pale as Anthony told him everything Ada had confessed. "I think I will be sick," he said as he leaned forward. He put his elbows on his desk and covered his face with his hands. "Why didn't she tell me?" he finally asked, not lifting his head.

"How can a daughter who loves her father tell him she had been forcibly taken, and that the scoundrel responsible also carved his initials into her back," Anthony said more as a statement than a question.

"And to think Agnes sent her to him. I can't believe it took me so long to see her for the wicked, heartless woman she was," said Thomas.

Anthony was quiet as he thought about what to do next. "I will be returning in a day or two. I want to put a couple of my men on

Randolph. The more I know about his actions, the safer she will be," he said.

"That is an excellent idea. I need you to be my eyes and ears, for I have not been a good father, and I'm afraid Ada needs a more capable protector." Thomas looked devastated.

"Sir, you have been a wonderful father. All men expect their children to be safe with their mothers. They don't expect their children to be put in harm's way by them. And most fathers would have turned out their daughters upon learning their reputations were ruined, but you did not. Instead, you gave Ada another chance, which was the right thing to do."

"You think so?" Thomas asked. He stared at Anthony with hope in his eyes.

"Yes, I do," said Anthony as he stood. "I will be taking my leave now. Try to be at ease, for I promise we will get this bastard," he said before exiting the room.

Thomas sat back and thought about what had happened to his daughter. He could not hold back the tears as they ran down his face.

Chapter Four

A couple of weeks passed, and everything was quiet. Randolph had yet to attempt to get to Ada. Anthony visited often and would take her to ride in the park or have tea.

Ada still would not attend social gatherings and refused to accept any visits from old friends, even when Charlotte and the two other girls apologized for what they'd done. After Henry had spoken to their fathers, they'd all quickly asked for forgiveness. In the end, Ada sent letters to each of them, telling them she held no grudges but preferred to be left alone.

"What have you been doing the last couple of days?" Anthony asked Ada as they sat on the sofa drinking tea.

"Father and I went to see Veronica's baby yesterday. She even let me hold her," Ada said with a big smile.

"So, she had a girl," said Anthony.

"Yes, she named her Leah after her mother. She is so beautiful," Ada said wistfully.

"You seem happy," Anthony said, noticing the glow in her eyes.

"Yes. Holding her baby, I realized how much I want to have a child of my own. I knew I would have children someday, but I thought I would do so more out of duty than desire. But holding that tiny person in my arms, I couldn't help but wonder what ours would look like," she said, looking down and blushing. Anthony put two fingers under her chin and raised her head, gently insisting that she look at him.

"They will be beautiful if they favor you," he said as he gazed upon her face. Slowly he leaned in then stopped, just before his lips touched hers. He didn't want to force intimacy upon her if she was not ready. He was happily surprised when she leaned closer to bridge the distance, and kissed him chastely. She pulled back and lowered her head, blushing again.

"We need to talk about the engagement," said Anthony. "In two months, let's announce our intent," he suggested.

"So soon?" Ada asked, surprised.

"You think it will be too soon? Are you worried about the scandal?" Anthony asked.

"I am afraid it doesn't matter. When we announce our engagement," she said, frowning, "there will be a scandal."

"Maybe so. Okay, we will wait three months," he said with a smile.

"Okay, we announce our engagement in three months," she giggled. *As if one more month would make a difference*, she thought with amusement.

* * *

The next day Anthony visited Henry.

"Anthony, to what do I owe this meeting? Has something happened?" Henry asked as they sat in his office.

"I have come to inform you that I will announce my engagement to Ada in three months," said Anthony.

"Malcolm has been telling people at White's that he is thinking about taking a wife soon," Henry said. He sat back in his chair, looking perturbed.

"I heard that. How did that scoundrel become a member of White's Gentlemen's Club anyway?" Anthony asked.

"I don't know. Bought, bribed, or blackmailed someone I imagine. It doesn't matter, for he is there, nonetheless. And once you announce your betrothal, I've no doubt he will make a move," said Henry.

Anthony was quiet for a moment. Finally he said, "I want you to know the truth about Ada and Randolph." It pained him to remember the look on Ada's face when she'd told him what had happened. He didn't relish the idea of betraying Ada's confidence, but it was imperative that Henry understand just how much of a threat Randolph was.

Henry was speechless after Anthony told him what Randolph had done to Ada. "Dear Lord. She didn't tell Thomas about this?" He asked finally. He pulled out a handkerchief and wiped his face.

"No, her mother told her not to say a word," said Anthony. He struggled to keep his voice devoid of emotion for Henry's sake, but inside he felt a simmering rage. He paused before continuing. "It seems she wanted Ada to forget about it. She told her bad things can happen sometimes, and all she could do was accept it."

"Mother of God. What a loving mother Agnes was," Henry said sarcastically, shaking his head. He was silent for a few moments, but Anthony could tell his mind working. Eventually, Henry opened the top drawer of his desk, pulled out a few papers, and handed them to Anthony.

"This is an investigation into Randolph. When did you have this done?" Anthony asked as he skimmed through the documents.

"My first wife was a brilliant woman. She purchased a bank and was there one day against my better judgment. A woman handling business went against my pride back then you see," Henry said, chuckling.

"I had forgotten you were married before," said Anthony.

"Yes, quite happily married," Henry said with a sad expression. "Leah was there one day when she overheard a conversation with a gentleman who wanted a line of credit. She told me something about the man did not settle well with her. It bothered her so much that she brought his information home and asked me to investigate him. As you can see, the man she'd asked me to look into was none other than Malcolm Randolph. But I had forgotten all about the report until he instigated these rumors."

"He was married before," Anthony said as he continued to read.

"Yes, his wife was the daughter of a wealthy tradesman. Right after they were married, her father's business partner met with an accident and died. Randolph then received a large dowry from his wife's father, and that's how he started his business. It was not a happy marriage for the girl by all accounts, but after receiving the dowry, Randolph acted the part of a doting husband," said Henry.

"It says she died from a riding accident," Anthony said, looking up at Henry.

"What was a woman who was four months pregnant doing on a horse?" Henry asked, leaning forward intently.

"You think he killed her?" Anthony asked, surprised.

"I do," answered Henry. "I think Randolph suddenly became a loving husband so no suspicion would fall on him. I haven't said any of this to Thomas because I did not know the truth about Ada. But now I think it's important that you and he both know Randolph's wife was Agnes's younger sister," he said.

"That's how Agnes knew Randolph," Anthony said.

Henry nodded his head, then said, "Anthony, Randolph is dangerous. More so than most people realize."

Anthony set the paperwork down on Henry's desk. "How are we going to handle this?" he asked.

"I have an idea," Henry answered, leaning forward again.

An hour later, Anthony left with a smile on his face. He was going to enjoy working with Henry. That man was not afraid of anything or anybody.

* * *

A few weeks later, Henry walked into White's and noticed Randolph playing cards with another gentleman. Standing to one side of the room, he chatted with some friends while watching and waiting for Randolph to finish playing. When the other man got up to leave, Henry excused himself from his friends and walked over to where Randolph sat.

Randolph was gathering his winnings when he noticed someone had sat down across from him. Looking up, he blanched when he realized it was Henry Aldridge. "Cambridge, you want to play a hand?" he asked, quickly recovering his composure.

"Not hardly. I heard a disturbing rumor that you were thinking about getting leg shackled," said Henry, his smile not quite reaching his eyes.

Randolph sat back, mirroring the other man's smile. "You already know whom I plan on marrying," he said.

"I would appreciate it if you left her alone. She has already suffered enough without being tied to you for the rest of her life," said Henry bluntly.

Randolph looked smug as he observed Henry. "Maybe I will. I heard Lady Veronica is divorcing," he said.

Henry's face showed no expression. Nobody liked playing cards with him because he was hard to read, but as Anthony watched the two men from where he sat in a corner across the room, he noticed Henry's hand clenched under the table. Rising swiftly to his feet, Anthony decided it was time to intercede.

"Excuse the interruption, gentleman. Henry, I would like to discuss some things with you, when you have time," Anthony said.

"We are finished here. I am free at this minute," Henry said, standing abruptly.

"Cambridge," Randolph said, nodding his head.

"Randolph," replied Henry curtly before turning his back on the man and following Anthony out of the room.

Once the door of the private room down the hall closed behind them, Henry picked up a chair and threw it at the wall.

"What did he say to put you in such a killing mood?" Anthony asked.

"That bastard dared to speak my daughter's name," Henry said. He closed his eyes and took several deep breaths.

"Why would he refer to her?" asked Anthony.

"He was implying that if he left Ada alone, he would try to marry Veronica," answered Henry.

"I am sorely confused. Veronica is already married," said Anthony.

"Veronica is divorcing," Henry said, his sadness replacing his anger.

"Oh," replied Anthony, surprised.

"And he just made a mistake. I only took her the papers today. Which means he must have eyes and ears in parliament," said Henry.

"That is good to know," Anthony said.

"He is probably paying for information," said Henry. "That's why we need to start removing his funds. I have purchased some of his debts and have also stopped a few of the proposals he made to some of my friends. He will start feeling the pinch soon," he added.

"I have people watching him in the event he decides to do something ignorant," said Anthony.

"Good," Henry said, taking another deep breath. Walking across the room, he picked up the chair and turned it upright. After inspecting it to be sure it was still sturdy, he then lowered himself into it.

"There is something I have been meaning to ask you, but I'm not sure if you'll want to talk about it," Anthony said as he too sat down.

"What is it?" Henry asked.

"I do not mean to bring up anything painful, or pry into your private life," Anthony said, unsure how to ask what was on his mind.

"You want to know how to love again," Henry said simply.

Anthony looked up, surprised the other man had read his mind so clearly.

"It was written all over your face the other day when I talked about Leah," Henry explained. He looked down as though gathering his thoughts before continuing. "I loved Leah with everything in me, but only after I stopped being a complete arse. My marriage was arranged, you see. I did not even meet her until we were married. I'm afraid I quite resented her at first," he said.

Anthony was shocked to learn such details about Henry's marriage. He waited silently for Henry to continue.

"But once I put aside my stupid pride, I realized what a treasure I'd been given. And when Leah died, I felt my soul had been ripped from my chest. I admire you for your ability to continue functioning after losing your wife and child together. My children were the only reason I was able to get up every morning following Leah's death," Henry said.

"But you found love again?" Anthony asked.

"Yes. Ellen was a blessing for us. Her husband died in battle six months after Leah passed. She was already helping with my children by that time, and they seemed to help her through her grief." Henry paused, then continued. "If I remember correctly, Veronica was three when Ellen and I decided to marry. I couldn't have asked for a better stepmother for my children. She is their mother in every way but blood. Then we had our son, Lucien. I was hesitant about having a child so late in life, but it has made my life all the better," he said.

Henry sat forward and rested his arms on the table. He looked Anthony directly in the eyes. "You will find love again, but you will never forget your first wife. The love and the memories will always be there. So, you will not be betraying her if you begin to have feelings for Ada," he said.

"Sometimes, I feel like I am torn between the two. I have developed a... fondness for Ada, and I feel guilty for it," Anthony said.

"That is normal. Don't let it cause you to miss out on being happy. I didn't know your late wife, but if you loved her, I know she was a good person. I'm sure she would want you to find someone and continue on with your life," Henry said.

It was Anthony's turn to take a deep, steadying breath. He stood up, causing Henry to do the same.

"Thank you for everything," Anthony said, holding out his hand.

"You are certainly welcome. My door is always open if you ever need to talk," Henry replied as he shook Anthony's hand.

"Right now, we have a bigger problem to manage," Anthony said as they walked towards the door.

"Without question. We must stay vigilant and keep our eyes open. Are you headed off to see Ada?" Asked Henry.

"Yes, I have been invited to supper. Thomas plans to bring a female guest over, and he thought it would be easier on Ada if I were there too," answered Anthony.

"That must be Meredith. Yes, Ada might benefit from your steadying presence," said Henry.

"You know Thomas's guest?" Anthony asked, curious.

"Yes," Henry answered with a twinkle in his eye. "Did you bring your carriage?" He asked.

"No, I didn't. I did not know how long I would be," answered Anthony.

"Let me give you a ride home, and I will fill you in. I think you should be aware of what you may be walking into this evening, so you are prepared," said Henry.

"Why do I get the feeling this is going to be an interesting dinner?" Anthony asked.

"You have no idea," chuckled Henry as they walked out.

* * *

Meredith arrived at the Claridge townhouse and was sitting in the dayroom when Thomas walked in. He smiled when he saw her. She stood up as he approached, and laughed as he pulled her in for an embrace.

"I can't tell you what it means to me that you are here," Thomas said, wrapping his arms around her.

Meredith leaned in briefly, enjoying the feel of his breath on her neck. Finally, she took a step back, forcing him to let go. "I am happy to be here too," she said, looking up at him with love in her eyes.

"I know I shouldn't say this, but I never stopped loving you," Thomas said as they sat down on the sofa next to one another.

"To be honest, neither did I. When I left for France, I thought my life was over. I was so angry and hurt. I did not think I would ever find happiness again. But I did. I married Count Edmond Herring," said Meredith.

"Did you love him?" Thomas asked, fearful of the answer. It hurt him to think that she had moved on after they lost touch, even though he had no right to feel that way. After all, he had married the woman who had ruined her, albeit unknowingly.

"I wouldn't call it love, but I was happy with him. He was kind and considerate and knew I wanted revenge for what had happened to me.

So he taught me how to obtain what I wanted, and when he died, he left me financially set," said Meredith.

"When did he die?" Asked Thomas.

"Five years ago," Meredith said. Her eyes took on a faraway look as she recalled the details of her past.

"Did you have any children?" Thomas asked, calling her attention back to the present.

"No. Edmond was in his late sixties when we married. He was lonely and just needed a companion. I was a good and attentive wife, and he listened to me. We would talk for hours about strategy. It was Edmond who taught me how to get revenge. He was a good man," she said.

"So you are Countess Herring?" Thomas asked.

"Dowager Herring," she said, reminding him she was a widow.

"Even though I am a little jealous, I am glad you found someone who made you happy," he said, taking both her hands into his own. The door opened, and they quickly separated, like young lovers caught in a tender moment.

Ada was stunned to see the beautiful woman sitting next to her father. She had blonde hair, and piercing blue eyes. When she smiled at Ada, it was genuine and warm, rather than simply polite. But as Meredith stood and began to approach her, Ada suddenly felt uneasy.

"Hello, Ada. I am Meredith," the woman said, still smiling. She stopped a few feet before Ada when she noticed her discomfort.

"Hello." Ada said, looking down. She did not know what to say. She had no idea how Meredith would act toward her, knowing it was her own mother who ruined her.

Without warning, Meredith reached out and wrapped her arms around Ada, embracing her as a mother would a child. Ada was utterly taken by surprise.

"It is a pleasure finally meeting you," Meredith said when she finally released Ada.

"It—it is a pleasure to meet you as well," responded Ada, still surprised by the warm introduction.

Thomas watched the two ladies, delighted that Meredith was trying to make Ada feel at ease.

* * *

Anthony sat in Henry's carriage, not knowing what to think. He was still stunned by Henry's account of what Agnes had done to Meredith.

"This Agnes woman was..." Anthony began. He didn't know what word to use that would best describe her.

"Evil?" Henry asked.

"Yes, that would be the appropriate word for her. I shouldn't be surprised. The ton is full of people who would not hesitate to destroy someone else to get what they wanted," said Anthony.

"Sadly, that is the truth," agreed Thomas. "However, I do know that since Agnes was removed from society and Ellen and her friends have had a more active role in it, most of the cruelty has waned," he said.

"That is good to know, especially since Ada will be back out in society once our engagement is announced," said Anthony.

"Yes, Ellen will be prepared to help ease her transition back into society when the time comes," Henry said.

"Thank you for letting me know. Ada will be relieved to know she has someone else on her side," Anthony said as the carriage came to a stop in front of the Claridge home. "Thank you, Henry, for everything. I don't know what would happen if you weren't helping us," he added.

"We still don't know what Randolph's next move will be, but I will be there to help in whatever way I can. A man like Randolph needs to face his reckoning," Henry said with a scowl.

Anthony nodded his head and left the carriage, making his way to the front door. He paused, thinking over everything he had learned from Henry. Taking a deep breath, he reached up and knocked on the door. It opened immediately. He was welcomed inside by a servant, who then led him to the dayroom. He immediately noticed Ada sitting on the sofa talking to a woman he did not recognize.

"Oh, Anthony, you're right on time," Thomas said as he walked up and shook his hand.

"Thank you for the invitation," responded Anthony. After exchanging pleasantries, he looked toward Ada, who was now looking at him with a bright smile. He thought about what Henry had said about allowing his feelings for Ada grow. As he and Thomas approached the ladies, they both stood.

"Meredith, this is Viscount Carlyle, Ada's soon-to-be husband. Anthony, this is Dowager Countess Herring," Thomas said, introducing them by their appropriate titles. He wanted to ensure Meredith was recognized by her standing, not her unpleasant past.

"It is a pleasure to meet you, Lord Carlyle," said Meredith.

Anthony bowed his head, and Meredith curtsied.

"The pleasure is mine, Lady Herring," said Anthony. Turning to Ada, he smiled and bowed his head. "Lady Ada," he said.

"Lord Carlyle," replied Ada as she dipped slightly.

Before anything more could be said, the butler appeared in the doorway. "Dinner is served," he announced.

"Come. Let us go and enjoy a delightful dinner," Thomas said. He held out his arm for Meredith. Anthony stayed back, wanting to talk to Ada before they went into to the dining room.

"How are things going?" he asked.

"Very well, thank you for asking," Ada said, still smiling. "Lady Herring is a lovely person. She's warm, and friendly, and very beautiful. I can see why my father fell in love with her." Her smile faded and she looked away as she thought about what her mother had done to her father.

"What's wrong? Did she say anything about your mother?" Anthony asked.

"You know about that?" Ada looked up at Anthony, surprised.

"Henry told me what your mother did to Meredith," he answered quietly.

Ada looked down, feeling tears forming in her eyes.

"Don't do that. You have no reason to feel embarrassed by what your mother did. That had nothing to do with you," Anthony said. Reaching out a hand, he lifted her head up so she would look at him. When their eyes met, Anthony saw the tears threatening to spill over onto her cheeks, and his heart hurt for her. He lowered his head slowly then stopped, wanting to ensure she was ready for such intimacy. Ada gazed at his mouth, gasping slightly at the thought of his lips on hers again. He took that as a yes and softly pressed his lips to hers. Ada slowly raised her arms and put them around his neck, causing Anthony to wrap his arms around her waist, pulling her closer to him.

At the sound of a cough, the two jumped apart, hastily putting a more modest distance between them. "Will you two be joining us?" Thomas asked from the doorway, his gaze averted.

"Yes, we were just discussing something of mutual interest," Anthony said. Turning slightly so his face was visible only to Ada, he winked. Then, with the poise of a perfect gentleman, he held his arm out for her. Her face crimson from blushing, Ada linked her arm with his and allowed him to lead her to the dining room. Thomas smiled as he watched them leave, sure he had walked in on something. Inside he was happy the two of them were getting closer.

* * *

The atmosphere at dinner was delightful as they listened to Meredith talk about her life in France. Some of the antics Meredith recounted about her stepson had caused several bursts of laughter to erupt at the table. Ada liked Meredith and was relieved she showed no malice towards her.

"Enough about me. Thomas told me about your upcoming announcement," Meredith said as the dinner plates were being cleared to make room for dessert. "I am so happy for you, Ada," she added with sincerity.

"Thank you. I couldn't have asked for a kinder man to come into my life," Ada said, smiling at Anthony. He smiled back at her.

"How was your day, Anthony?" Thomas asked, changing the subject abruptly.

"It was a normal business day. I did run into Henry this afternoon at the club, and he informed me Veronica and her husband are divorcing," said Anthony.

"I was hoping they would have decided not to divorce," Meredith said, looking down at her hands.

"You knew they intended to divorce?" Thomas asked.

"Yes," said Meredith quietly.

Anthony looked across the table Ada. Her cheeks were wet with tears.

"Ada?" Anthony said, concerned.

"It's my fault," she said. She delicately dabbed at her face with a lace handkerchief she'd extracted from the sleeve of her dress.

Meredith stood and walked around the grand table to sit beside her. "Ada, look at me," she said, waiting for Ada to look up. When she knew she had Ada's full attention, she said, "What happened was not all your fault."

"Veronica has been so good to me. If she can forgive me, I don't understand why she cannot forgive Owen so they can be a happy family. It is I who ruined her life." Unable to hold back the flood of tears any longer, Ada began to sob.

Meredith enfolded the shaking girl in her arms, offering motherly comfort as Ada cried. She looked over Ada's head at Thomas, who looked bewildered as to what he should do. With the tilt of her head, she conveyed to him that she would handle things with Ada privately.

"Anthony, let us retire to the study," Thomas said with a barely concealed look of relief. He stood and motioned for the footman to also leave. Anthony followed Thomas out of the room, glancing back once before the footman closed the door behind them.

Meredith smiled inwardly to see the swiftness with which the men exited the room, before turning her attention back to the sobbing girl.

It took a few moments for Ada to stop crying, but finally, she sat up and dried her tears with her handkerchief.

Meredith waited until Ada had recovered her composure before speaking. "Ada, I hope you will take what I say next to heart," she said. At Ada's nod, she continued. "Ellen has confided much in me, and I believe she would not mind if I shared some perspective with you. You must understand it was Owen who broke Veronica's trust, not you. It was his mistake, not yours. I know you deeply regret your actions, but Owen is the one who violated his wedding covenant, not you. And after he broke Veronica's trust, he could never get it back. Now Veronica wishes to start over in Scotland and it is for the best. She has a real chance at happiness there. I know she would not want you to blame yourself anymore. You have changed, and she is happy you have a chance at a good life. In time, Owen will move on and find someone else eventually. And don't forget Veronica already has the love of her life in her arms."

Ada looked up at Meredith with a half-smile. "Yes, her daughter is a beautiful little love," she said.

"You must accept how things are and go on with your life. It's time to forgive yourself," Meredith said.

"Why are you being so nice to me after what my mother did to you?" Ada asked, looking genuinely curious.

"You are not your mother, and I won't judge you based on her transgressions. You were her child, and you looked to her for guidance, as any child would," Meredith said, reaching out to squeeze Ada's hand reassuringly before continuing. "It is my hope that we can become good friends, but true friendship is based on trust. So, I am not going to hide anything from you. Including why I'm here this evening. The truth is, I have always loved your father, and I am grateful to say he still loves me as well." Meredith paused a moment to allow her words to sink in. Straightening her shoulders, she then asked, "Would you have a problem if your father and I were to marry one day?"

Ada did not hesitate in her response. "No. I want my father to be happy," she said with sincerity. It was her turn to reach out and squeeze Meredith's hand and smile.

"Good. Now let's put all this behind us and rejoin our men," Meredith said. The two ladies stood and turned to leave. "I pray you won't think it amiss if I say that your man is a fine specimen indeed…" Meredith said with a wink as they exited the room, which caused Ada to giggle.

* * *

Anthony had been pacing the study floor for what felt like hours, though the mantle clock indicated only a quarter hour had passed. He was angry at himself for not realizing the topic of Veronica's divorce would upset Ada.

Thomas observed Anthony's agitation, not saying a word. Truth be told, it put him at ease to see Anthony worrying about Ada. Anthony stopped mid-stride, and the two men turned their attention to the ladies as they entered the room.

"I'm sorry for my outburst," Ada said as she crossed the room to stand in front of Anthony.

"No, it is I who is sorry. I wasn't thinking," Anthony responded. He lowered his head, not able to look into her eyes.

"You could not know my feelings on the subject. It is not your fault. And I am fine now," Ada said. She tentatively reached out to touch his hand. Surprised by her touch, Anthony looked up to sees her smiling at him. He could not help but smile back.

Meredith and Thomas watched the interaction with interest. Looking across the room at each other, they shared a smile of their own.

Chapter Five

A few months passed, and Anthony and Ada's engagement was announced, along with that of Thomas and Meredith.

Meredith's return to society caused more scandal than Ada's engagement. Ada and Anthony surmised that Meredith had deliberately timed things that way to keep the attention off Ada. And it worked. Tongues wagged and gossip columns speculated fervently, especially about Meredith's marriage to the wealthy count who had left her his fortune.

Even Meredith's parents, who had previously turned their backs on her, now reached out. Although Meredith finally agreed to meet with her mother, theirs was not a warm reunion. In truth, Meredith wanted nothing to do with either of them after how they had treated her. She knew their motivation for contacting her now was only because they'd learned of the wealth and power she'd acquired.

At first, her mother had feigned remorsefulness, blaming her father for casting Meredith out with nothing. But once she realized Meredith saw through her, the facade fell, and the heartless woman Meredith had known growing up reappeared.

Thomas shared with Ada what had transpired when Meredith reunited with her mother. It made Ada reflect on her own situation. She could not imagine what she would have done in Meredith's shoes. She loved her father even more for not disowning her when her reputation had been publicly ruined. She and Meredith had become fast friends over the last few months, and she felt blessed that things were going so wonderfully.

* * *

In a seedy tavern along the docks, one man was livid when he learned of Ada's engagement. Taking his liberties with a barmaid proved to be a short-lived, albeit pleasant distraction. Having left her in the room bloody, bruised, and barely conscious, Malcolm Randolph's attitude had improved somewhat, but he was still angry. He could not afford the time it would take to cause sufficient trouble for Anthony or Ada. At least not yet. Right now he had to focus on saving his finances from ruin. He knew someone was coming after him, and in his mind, it could only be Henry Aldridge.

Randolph knew he should not have goaded the other man about his daughter that day, but he'd been unable to stop himself. He loathed Aldridge and his supercilious attitude. Randolph's illegal endeavors were keeping his bills paid, but were not leaving him with any extra. It infuriated him to not be able to stop Ada's engagement; he'd thought her fortune had been his for the taking following her public humiliation. He thought back to his first encounter with Ada and licked his lips. She had been a tasty morsel to be sure, and taming her would have been a most pleasant diversion. But he would bide his time, making everyone believe he had given up. Then he would strike. If it meant getting rid of Carlyle, he would do that. It wouldn't be the first time he'd orchestrated someone's fatal accident. In time, Henry would think he had won, and he would stop interfering with Randolph's business dealings. If Randolph was anything, he was a patient man.

* * *

One evening during dinner with Ada and Anthony, Thomas announced that he and Meredith had set their wedding date for two months hence.

"But that's not enough time to prepare!" Ada said with dismay.

"We don't want a big affair, just close family and friends. Besides, I have you to help me get ready for it," Meredith said, smiling at Ada.

"You want my help? I thought you would have Lady Ellen assist you with the preparations," Ada said, surprised.

"Ellen will certainly help, but I would like you to be involved as well. Your opinion is important to me," Meredith said.

"I would be honored to be of assistance any way I can," Ada said, smiling.

Anthony was pleased that Ada finally had a woman in her life who would be a good role model. When Ada looked at him, he nodded encouragingly.

"Are you inviting Veronica?" Ada asked, turning her attention back to Meredith.

"Yes, she will be invited, but Ellen has advised me she will be unable to attend. She is hosting something called 'the hunt'," Meredith said.

"Ah, so she is bringing that back," Thomas said with interest, sitting back in his chair.

"What is 'the hunt'?" Anthony asked, his interest piqued.

"It was something her grandfather did every year. Before the bitter winter, people from miles around would gather at the castle in anticipation of the event. The men would hunt for two days and bring back whatever game they caught. The women would process the meat as it was received, and then it would be divided up. When the hunt was finished, everyone would leave with enough meat to supply them through the winter."

"What an excellent idea," Anthony said. "Er, did you say castle?" He added, raising one eyebrow.

"Yes, Veronica inherited her grandfather's castle," Thomas said, chuckling.

"A beautiful, enormous castle," Ada said, spreading her arms wide to emphasize its incredible size, which caused everyone to laugh.

"Getting back to the subject of our wedding," Meredith said, looking at Thomas, then at Ada. "I think everything is settled for the time being. I will confer with Ellen and set up a day to finalize the details," she said.

Anthony enjoyed seeing Ada looking so happy. Over the last few months, he and Ada had been growing increasingly close. She had even permitted him to steal a few kisses from her here and there. He realized his feelings for her were evolving into what might be considered love. But while things were progressing well with their relationship, he was still worried about Randolph. The man had been conspicuously quiet of late. And when a man like Randolph was quiet, it brooked concern. He knew it was not a matter of whether Randolph made his move, rather, of when. Anthony was resolved to remain on guard, no matter how long it took.

Ada was surprised when she and Meredith visited the modiste to discuss the design of Meredith's wedding dress. Ellen was there, as expected. But Ada had not expected Eleanor and Hannah to also be in attendance. Eleanor was friendly, but Hannah remained distant with Ada during the visit. Although she was not rude, she was not warm either. Sensing the tension, Meredith did everything she could to make Ada feel at ease, even asking her opinion from time to time.

As they were finalizing things and preparing to leave, three young ladies entered the shop. Ada tensed immediately as she recognized Charlotte, Rose, and Penelope standing by the door. Although they'd each sent letters of apology to her begging forgiveness for their actions, Ada knew they had only done so under pressure from their parents. She was not naïve enough to believe they'd been sincere. And she had no doubt they still harbored ill feelings towards her.

The memory of the horrible night they had attacked her came rushing back to Ada. When the three ladies noticed Ada, they exchanged conspiratorial glances. Together, they smiled at Ada and began to approach, which caused Ada to reflexively move closer to Eleanor.

Hannah had not put much effort into hiding how she felt about spending time with Ada. If her mother had not withheld the fact Ada would be there, she would have made up an excuse not to come. But she'd been surprised at Ada's demeanor. Gone was her selfish arrogance and self-absorbed chatter. This was not the same Ada she had once despised.

Hannah noticed Ada suddenly move to stand beside her mother, which puzzled her. She knew something wasn't right when she saw the fearful look on Ada's face. Following Ada's gaze she knew it had something to do with the three girls walking toward her. Although she wasn't sure what was happening, she did not like how Ada seemed to cower in their presence. It triggered a feeling of protectiveness within her. Walking over to Ada, she stood next to her, positioning herself in such a way that she could subtly shield Ada with her body. Eleanor, who also noticed the girls approach, reached out to take Ada's hand, squeezing it reassuringly.

Ellen and Meredith were still in the changing room, unaware of what was happening. Ada was surprised when Hannah moved to stand closer to her. And when Eleanor held her hand she relaxed. Without saying a word, both ladies had let her know they would protect her.

"Hello, Lady Eleanor, Hannah, Ada," said Charlotte in a falsely sweet voice. It was impossible for anyone to miss the sour tone she used when she said Ada's name. Charlotte seemed emboldened, but the other two girls now appeared to be uncomfortable and refused to make eye contact with anyone.

"What are you girls up to today?" Eleanor asked politely.

"We are doing some shopping. We saw Ada through the window, and decided to congratulate her on her upcoming wedding," Charlotte answered. Although her voice remained sweet, her eyes betrayed the harshness of her words. "Her father has managed to find her a handsome, upstanding husband. That must have been quite a feat," said Charlotte. She stared at Ada, no longer trying to conceal her contempt.

Hannah had not gotten over what Ada had done to Veronica, but she despised Charlotte. "Yes, Ada has gained the love of a very good man. They are very happy together," she said. She knew how much her words would irritate Charlotte, who thrived on the misfortune of others. "Have you received any offers of marriage yet, Charlotte," Hannah asked with mock innocence, not bothering to hide her smile.

Charlotte appeared to blanch for an instant, but recovered swiftly and smiled back at her. "Yes, I have recently received a couple of new proposals. I am still deciding whether to accept either of them," she said with an airy wave of her hand. "Now if you will excuse us, we need to be on our way," she said. She knew she'd find no more sport with Ada while the other two ladies were there to protect her.

"Yes, of course," Eleanor said. The three girls curtsied to Eleanor, nodded to Hannah and Ada, then left the shop.

"Thank you," whispered Ada, not looking up.

"You don't need to fear them anymore. They will never harm you again," Eleanor responded in an equally hushed tone, not wanting anyone to overhear.

Hannah wondered what those girls had done to Ada. *It must not have been good for mother to be this protective*, she thought.

Before Hannah could ask any questions, Ellen and Meredith came out of the dressing room. "I think we've accomplished what we set out to do today. Thank you all for your help, this has been a wonderful experience," Meredith said. Her cheeks were flushed with happiness as she looked around the room at her friends. Her smile faltered when she noticed Ada's countenance, but she did not say anything.

Ada was quiet on the carriage ride home. Meredith finally confronted her when they entered the house. "What's wrong?" She asked, her voice full of concern.

Ada could not hold back from telling her what had happened any longer. "While you and Lady Ellen were in the dressing room, Charlotte, Rose, and Penelope came into the dress shop," she said, looking down at the floor.

"Did they say anything to you?" Meredith asked sharply.

"Lady Eleanor and Hannah protected me from them," Ada said with wonder. "Charlotte was her usual condescending self, full of false politeness and malicious intent," she added, her expression darkening. She quickly told Meredith what had happened.

"They are just jealous. Don't pay any attention to what anyone has to say. All you need to worry about is what Anthony thinks. I do believe that man is falling in love with you," Meredith said.

Meredith's revelation served its intended purpose. Ada forgot all about the incident at the modiste's shop and looked at her with a surprised but hopeful expression.

"Do you think so?" Ada asked.

"Yes, I do. Now go on up to your room and get changed for supper," said Meredith as she shooed Ada towards the stairs.

"Yes, mother," Ada said automatically, not realizing what she'd just said. She traipsed up the stairs, the drama of the day now replaced with thoughts of her betrothed.

Meredith stood at the bottom of the stairs, stunned. She didn't notice Thomas walking over to stand beside her.

"Did I hear right?" Thomas asked.

Meredith turned to face him with tears in her eyes. "She called me mother," she said, her voice cracking.

"Yes, she did," Thomas said, wrapping his arms around her. He couldn't remember when he'd felt as happy as he was in that moment. His family was finally whole.

* * *

Meredith stood beside Thomas as they said their vows. The church was filled with family and friends, and everyone could see the love they had for each other. Ada sat in the front pew with Anthony, who discretely held her hand. From time to time, they would catch each other's gaze and smile. Anthony could see the love in Ada's eyes, and it warmed his heart.

* * *

In the back of the church Angelique Beauchamp sat alone. She was a known mistress to some of the peerage. When the service ended and everyone else left to attend the wedding breakfast, Angelique remained behind. When Meredith noticed her, she led Thomas over to introduce them. Angelique stood up gracefully as they approached, and Meredith embraced her affectionately.

"Thomas, this is Angelique Beauchamp, my dear friend."

"It is a pleasure to meet you," Thomas said with a bow.

"The pleasure is mine, my lord," Angelique said with a heavy French accent.

"I am so happy you made it. Will you be attending the breakfast?" Meredith asked.

"No. It would not be appropriate. I shouldn't have come today, but I wanted to see your wedding," Angelique said apologetically.

"I don't care what other people say. You have been my friend for a few years now, and I value that friendship," Meredith said as she took Angelique's hand.

"And I value yours as well, *mon cher*," said Angelique. "If you ever need me, I will be there for you. But now that you have returned and are a member of the *beau monde*, you must be careful about the company you keep. In the eyes of the ton, and I am not someone you should associate with," she said.

"You are welcome to visit me in my home anytime. Polite society be damned. You were there for Meredith when she needed help, and I will never forget that," Thomas said.

"Thank you, my lord. But we both know that cannot happen," said Angelique. She looked at Meredith fondly, and squeezed her hand. "You are a dear friend, and I will never forget you," she said.

A tear rolled down Meredith's face as the two women hugged once more. "I'm afraid we should take our leave now, as our guests will be waiting," Meredith said with regret. She and Thomas walked to the doors of the church. At the exit, Meredith stopped and looked back at her friend one last time. "Thank you for everything. I couldn't have made it without your help. You deserve so much more than the life you have been dealt. If there is ever a time when you need me, all you need to do is ask," she said. Turning her attention back to Thomas, the two proceeded out the doors, leaving the church, and Angelique, behind.

"I'm sorry," Thomas said when he and Meredith were settled in their carriage.

Meredith smiled at her new husband, grateful for his compassion. "I will miss her, but she is right. I wouldn't care if it was just me, but I must think of you and Ada. With everything Ada has been through, she finally has some peace in her life. I cannot risk jeopardizing that for my own selfish reasons," she said.

"I love you," Thomas said as he held her close.

"I know," Meredith answered, snuggling closer still.

* * *

After the wedding breakfast was over and the guests had left, Anthony said his goodbyes. There were pressing business matters that needed his attention. But when he returned home and seated himself at his desk, he found he could not get Ada off his mind. No matter how hard he tried, he still felt as if he was betraying his dead wife's memory.

Feeling restless, he got up and left to visit Genevieve's grave. Once there, he sat down and traced the etchings of her stone with his hand. Although he felt a little strange doing so, he began talking to her stone, opening up about what was on his mind. He needed to decide whether to let his feelings grow for Ada. Needing an answer, he prayed for some sort of sign to let him know what he should do. Finally, he got up, brushing leaves from his trousers. He felt disappointed and a little bit silly for thinking he might actually get an answer. Shaking his head, he turned to leave, then noticed an older man holding a shovel, standing next to him.

"Pardon my intrusion, young man, but I couldn't help overhearing your conversation," the older man said.

"That's quite all right. Do we know each other? You seem very familiar to me." Anthony asked, looking closely at the man.

"No, we have never met. But, if you don't mind me telling you a story, it might help your situation," the older man said as he leaned on his shovel.

"Okay," Anthony said, not wanting to be rude to the stranger.

"I was married to the most beautiful girl once upon a time. We were young and very much in love. She was my world, but she died giving birth to my second son. When she died, I felt like my life had also ended," the older man said. He paused as his eyes glazed over, "The thought of loving anyone else never occurred to me. But one day, I did meet someone new, and discovered I had feelings for her. I felt guilty for moving on."

As the older man talked, Anthony turned back and looked at Genevieve's grave. "What did you do?" Anthony asked.

"The same thing you are doing now. I asked my late wife if it was okay," said the older man.

"Did you get an answer?" Asked Anthony.

"Yes, she sent someone to tell me I had her blessing, and that she was happy I had found someone to love again. That's why I am here, Anthony," said the older man.

It took Anthony a second to realize the man had used his given name. He turned back to the man to ask him how he'd known his name, then froze. The older man was no longer there. He looked around, searching for the man, to no avail. The graveyard was deserted. He looked back at his wife's grave, trying to make sense of what had just happened. "That was strange," he said aloud. He looked at Genevieve's grave one last time and smiled before softly walking away.

Chapter Six

It had been a few months since the wedding, and Ada and her family were enjoying dinner together, chatting about the day.

"Ellen delivered our invitation to Veronica's wedding," Meredith said.

"She is getting remarried?" Ada asked, surprised.

"Yes, she is marrying the grandson of a Highland Lord. Ellen said she had never seen Veronica so happy."

"When is it?" Thomas asked.

"Next month. We should make arrangements to attend," said Meredith.

"I don't think it would be appropriate for me to go," Ada said, looking down.

"She has included you in the invitation," said Meredith.

"I am not surprised, but it would be in bad form for me to attend. I was the reason her first marriage ended, after all," Ada said quietly.

"I don't know if we should leave you alone," said Thomas, looking conflicted.

"I will be fine, don't worry. I won't go anywhere unaccompanied. And don't forget, I have Anthony looking out for me. But you and mother must go. Veronica has accepted the invitation to my upcoming wedding, so it would not look good if you did not attend hers," said Ada.

"You are right. All right, as long as you are sure you will be careful," Thomas said.

"I'm sure," Ada said, smiling at her father.

* * *

After dinner, Meredith and Ada retired to the drawing room to work on their embroidery.

"What has you so distracted?" Meredith asked when she noticed Ada had stopped sewing and was staring at the fire, deep in thought.

Ada set her embroidery down and took a deep breath. "I'm scared," she said, looking at Meredith.

"About what?" Meredith asked, setting her own embroidery down. She leaned forward in her chair, he eyes full of concern.

"What if I can't... be with Anthony?" Ada blurted. Seeing the surprise on Meredith's face, she continued. "I mean, what if I cannot stand to be intimate with him?" she asked, tears beginning to well up in her eyes.

Meredith nodded with sympathy, now understanding Ada's concern. "It is normal to have some anxiety," she said. "If I may be so bold, let me ask you this... I know you two have kissed. So how do you feel when Anthony is close to you?" she asked gently.

"It feels like my hair is standing up on the back of my neck. I cannot think clearly. And I love it when he puts his arms around me. It makes me feel safe," Ada answered honestly.

"Then why do you feel you can't be intimate with him?" Meredith asked.

"Every time I think about... *that*... with Anthony, Malcolm Randolph's face comes to mind and then I remember what he did to me. I know it is all just in my head, but I can't help but worry. I have started having nightmares again," said Ada.

"Have you talked to Anthony about how you feel?" Meredith asked.

"No. Do you think I should?" asked Ada.

"I think it might be a good idea, but only if you feel comfortable talking to him," Meredith said.

"I am unsure I know how to tell him my fears," Ada said.

Meredith fell silent, looking thoughtful. Ada had become accustomed to Meredith over the past year, and could tell she was weighing the merits of an idea in her head. So Ada didn't say anything. She just waited.

"Your father and I will be in Scotland at Veronica's wedding for at least a fortnight. That would be the perfect time to… determine whether you have any issues to work out," Meredith said, a look of mischief on her face.

"I don't think father would approve," Ada said, unsure if Meredith was saying what she thought she was saying. She wondered what Meredith was up to.

"Oh, posh. I will discuss the matter with your father. I'm sure I can explain things in such a way that he will be perfectly okay with it. Besides, it will give us something to discuss on the way to Scotland," Meredith said as she got up to leave. She stopped suddenly, then turned to face Ada. "On second thought, perhaps don't say anything to Anthony just yet. There is still a month before your father and I leave. I expect that should provide me with enough time to get everything arranged," she said. Walking over to Ada, she leaned down to kiss her on the forehead. "Please don't worry about any of this," she said, then turned and left the room.

It took a few seconds for Meredith's words to sink in. That meant Meredith wouldn't tell her father until they had left for the wedding. Ada couldn't help but smile, and feel a rush of love for her beautiful stepmother. For the first time in her life, Ada felt like she had a mother who put her happiness first. Not her own social standing, or strategy, or what she herself stood to gain from things. Just Ada's happiness.

* * *

Two weeks later, Anthony and Ada were strolling through the garden when Meredith found them. "Ada, would you please give me a moment alone with Anthony?" she said.

"Of course," said Ada, quickly excusing herself.

Anthony was surprised that Meredith wished to speak to him alone, and wondered if he'd done something wrong.

"Don't look so nervous," Meredith said with a laugh, which put him somewhat at ease. "I need to speak to you about something Ada told me. This is a delicate topic so please forgive me my forwardness. Simply put, she is nervous about the wedding night," she said, getting straight to the point.

Anthony was shocked that Meredith would talk to him about something so private. "Why hasn't she said something to me?" He finally asked.

"She is fearful that what... happened to her... might affect her ability to be intimate," said Meredith. She stifled the urge to smile at Anthony's look of surprise. "In light of this, I think it might be a good idea for the two of you to get a little... closer... before the wedding. Knowing her fears were groundless would certainly ease her mind," she said, maintaining a straight face.

"What do you have in mind?" Anthony asked, his shock now replaced with interest. It was his turn to try not to smile.

"Thomas and I will be leaving to attend Veronica's wedding tomorrow. That would be the perfect opportunity for you to discuss this matter," said Meredith.

"An excellent idea. If it puts Ada at ease, I would be happy to discuss the subject with her," said Anthony. He couldn't hold back the smile any longer.

"Good. I knew you would understand. I will fetch Ada now so the two of you may continue your visit. And don't worry, everything will be arranged before we leave," said Meredith.

Anthony watched Meredith walk away, thinking Thomas's life would never be dull with her around. When Ada returned, her face was red, and she seemed unable to look at him. He put both hands on the sides of her face and gently tilted her head up. "Are you not attracted to me Ada?" he asked softly.

Ada's eyes widened in surprise. "Y-y-yes, of course I am," she answered.

Anthony found the blush that rose from her neckline and spread across her face to be most becoming. "Do you believe that I am attracted to you as well?" he asked. Ada nodded, her blush deepening.

"Then why would you be concerned about the two of us becoming closer... in the romantic sense?" Anthony asked.

"I don't know why. I just get scared when I think about us being together," Ada said, looking miserable.

"Ada, it is completely understandable for you to feel this way. What happened to you was not something you can simply forget," said Anthony. He did not want to push, but Meredith's words were still on his mind. "Do you want me to come over when your parents leave for Scotland?" He asked. He so wanted her to say yes. Thoughts of Ada, and his desire for her, were increasingly on his mind the closer they got to their wedding. He had broken off all contact with his former lovers as soon as Ada had accepted his proposal. All he wanted now was to be with her.

"Yes," Ada said shyly, holding her breath. She hoped he wanted to be with her as well.

"I have wanted to be with you for some time now." Anthony said, answering her unspoken question. He lowered his head and kissed her lips softly, mindful that Ada's lady's maid was watching.

As Anthony pulled back, they gazed at each other, unwilling to break the connection. For an instant, Ada felt sure she saw love in his eyes. Her heart skipped a beat, and she felt it might burst from happiness.

"I must take my leave of you now, as I have some pressing business to attend to," Anthony said finally. "But I will see you soon," he said, kissing her forehead before departing.

When Anthony returned home, later that evening, he found a letter waiting for him.

Come to the rear entrance at ten o'clock tomorrow night. Lucy will be waiting.

Anthony smiled. Meredith would have made a good spy. He went up the stairs two at a time, feeling excited. Once inside his bedroom, he stopped short, realizing he needed to figure out his approach for the following evening. Ada would need him to take it slow. He could not afford to lose control and risk scaring her. Anthony still couldn't help but smile. He knew Ada would be okay, and that she loved him. She hadn't said it yet, but he saw it in her eyes, and he realized he might love her too.

The next day, Anthony tried to stay busy and keep his mind off of his upcoming rendezvous with Ada. Finally abandoning hope of getting any work done, he sat back in his chair and allowed his mind to fill with the thoughts of his betrothed. Before he knew it, the sun was setting, and he realized he would have to hurry if he hoped to make it to the Claridge home by 10 o'clock. He bathed in a rush, then spent an uncharacteristic amount of time deciding which pants, shirt, and cravat Ada might like best. Flustered, he made himself stop and take a deep breath. He hadn't been this nervous since his first night with Genevieve. He knew it wasn't necessary to go to such lengths to impress Ada—she had already agreed to marry him after all. Still, something inside him compelled him to try. *What am I doing? This is ridiculous. I feel like a young buck about to experience his first mating season,* he thought.

* * *

As his carriage neared Ada's place, it slowed to a stop. He'd asked the coachman to drop him off a couple of houses away for the sake of discretion. After stepping out of the carriage, he took a quick survey of his surroundings then proceeded to walk the rest of the way. Once there, he looked around to be sure nobody was watching, then slipped through the gate, making his way around the side of the house. He stopped dead in his tracks when he heard the sound of a pistol being cocked.

"What are you doing here?" growled an unfamiliar voice. Anthony knew it wasn't Aaron, which worried him.

"I'm Anthony Carlyle checking on my betrothed," said Anthony in an assertive voice.

"Captain? I wasn't expecting you tonight. You must be missing your lady something awful," the other voice said, sounding far less menacing.

Anthony turned around. Even in the low light, he recognized the man standing before him. "William?" He asked.

"Good to finally talk to you. Staying in the shadows makes for a boring time," The other man said with a broad smile as he reached out to shake Anthony's hand.

"Why are you here? I thought Aaron was guarding Ada," said Anthony.

"We are both here since Lord and Lady Aldridge, and Lord and Lady Claridge have departed for Scotland to attend Lady Veronica's wedding. Lord Aldridge thought Randolph might try to seize the opportunity to get to Ada while everyone was away," William said.

The two men turned suddenly at the sound of a snapping branch. "I forgot to tell William you would be visiting tonight," Aaron said as he stepped out of the shadows.

"You know?" Anthony asked.

"We hear more secrets in the shadows than the ladies of the ton do. And I understand completely why you are here. My heart goes out to Lady Ada. I will explain everything to William," said Aaron as he patted William on the shoulder.

"Thank you," said Anthony. He began walking towards the back of the townhouse then stopped and turned around. "I want you both to know that I will sleep soundly at night knowing who is here," he said. With that he turned back towards the house and continued walking, finally disappearing out of sight.

When Anthony reached the back door, he knocked once lightly. Immediately it opened a tiny crack, then wider as Lucy stepped back to let him in.

"This way, my Lord," she whispered as she led him down the hall and up the stairs to a door on the left. She stopped, pointed, and curtsied before walking away.

Anthony knocked lightly, and the door opened. Ada's head peeked cautiously around it, presumably to confirm it was him. Smiling tentatively, she backed up to let him enter. He smiled in return as he stepped into the room, closing the door softly behind him. He looked around at his new surroundings, giving both of them time to adjust to his presence in her bedroom. The fireplace was lit, and one lamp burned on the bedside table, lending the room a warm, welcoming glow.

Anthony walked over to one of the chairs situated in front of the fire and removed his overcoat, placing it over the chairback.

Wondering why Ada was so quiet, he turned to find her still standing by the door, looking down at the floor. His breath caught in his throat as he looked at her. She was wearing nothing but her shift, and while it was modest by any standard, the fact that it was all she had on caused his manhood to grow.

Slowly he walked towards her until he stood so close she could feel the heat radiating from his body. Ada leaned forward slightly to lay her head against his chest. Instinctively Anthony wrapped his arms around her, pulling her even closer against him. Ada raised her head looking deeply into his eyes. She could see his yearning and wondered if her eyes reflected her feelings as well.

Lowering his head, Anthony captured her lips in a kiss that betrayed his growing desire. Stepping back, he gently pulled her with him as he moved towards the bed, never releasing her mouth. When they reached the bed he pulled back slightly, smiling at her whimper of protest. Reaching down, he grasped the hem of her shift with both hands, then slowly raised it up and over her head. Tossing it to the floor, he then gathered her into his arms and gently laid her on the bed.

"Beautiful," he said, his eyes hungrily drinking in her nakedness. Ada immediately reached down to cover herself, feeling suddenly shy. He clasped her wrists gently, raising them up to rest against the pillows as he leaned in for another slow kiss. He began stroking her face and arms as their kiss deepened, and Ada's arms crept up to encircle his neck, pulling him tighter against him. Feeling the flames of his desire burn stronger at her response, he stood quickly to remove his shirt and the rest of his clothes.

Ada watched him as he returned to the bed and stretched himself out beside her. She raised her hand to gently cup the side of his face.

Anthony looked at her, and was dismayed to see tears glistening in her eyes. "Why are you crying? Do you need to stop?" He asked with concern as he sat up on one elbow.

"No. Being here like this with you feels right. I'm not scared anymore. I think it's because I—I love you," Ada said in a breathless rush.

That was all he needed to hear. Moving closer to her, he pressed his body against her for a heated kiss. She gasped as Anthony's hands roamed over her body, forgetting everything but the feel of his touch and the fire it ignited deep within her. Everywhere he touched seemed to burn her. She had never felt such a strong need for a man before.

Could it be because of my feelings for him? She wondered. She knew what it was to feel a man's loving touch, but this was quite different. Although she'd cared for Jeremy and Owen, her former lovers, she had not loved them. As Anthony's lips seared her neck, she let go of all thoughts of the past, focusing only on who she was with now. Her hands began to explore his body. She let them travel over his arms, chest, back, and everywhere else they wanted to go.

Her back arched as he took one, then her other nipple in his mouth, suckling, and nipping skillfully. He began to kiss and lick his way down her body until he reached the apex between her legs. His own arousal intensified at the sound of her moans as his tongue concentrated on the secret bud nestled within her exquisite flower. He refused to stop until she cried out his name and her body convulsed.

Only then did Anthony slowly move up the length of her quivering body and position himself at her entrance. Gently, he laid his body on top of hers, resting most of his weight on his elbows. Gazing at her flushed cheeks, he moved a stray hair out of her face, then waited until she opened her eyes and looked at him. Slowly he pushed his member inside her, never losing eye contact. When Ada instinctively wrapped her legs around his hips and met his thrusts, Anthony lost what little restraint he had left. It wasn't long before they both climaxed, and Anthony collapsed on top of Ada, lost in the moment. Ada wrapped her arms around him tenderly, breathing in his masculine scent. She'd never realized the difference it made when you loved the person you were with.

* * *

It was dark in the graveyard, save for the moon's slender crescent, which illuminated the tombstone from behind. The older man who had spoken to Anthony when he'd last visited, now approached a woman with long blonde hair. The woman's face was turned away, so he saw only her back. He could tell she held something in her arms.

"He's going to be okay," said the old man, coming to stand beside the woman.

"Do you hear that, sweetheart? Your papa is going to be okay," the woman said to the swaddled bundle she held close. "It's time, grandfather," she said, turning her attention back to the old man. The woman held out one hand, and the old man clasped it, then the two began walking towards the moonbeam. Before they stepped into its light, the woman turned her head and looked back with a smile. Anthony gasped, and his eyes flew open.

"Genevieve," he whispered. A tear slid down his face. It had just been a dream, but it felt like a weight had been lifted off him. As he replayed the details of the scene in his mind, he froze. "Grandfather," he repeated out loud. He remembered seeing a painting of his late wife's grandparents. He realized with a start that the old man he'd met in the graveyard had been the man in that painting. He could not explain it, but he knew somehow the dream had been real—as real as the man he'd met that day. And he knew now, without a doubt, that Genevieve had stayed to look out for him.

He looked down at Ada, snuggled up next to him, sound asleep. *Genevieve must know that Ada loves me, or she wouldn't have left*, he thought. He knew that Genevieve was finally at rest, and that now he could move on. He was free to love Ada, knowing he had Genevieve's blessing. This thought eased something inside of him. He looked up at the ceiling whispering his thanks, then he closed his eyes and drifted off into a peaceful sleep.

Chapter Seven

A fortnight after her wedding, Veronica sat on her sofa, wrapped in the arms of her adoring husband, Sean. She was attempting to read a letter from her mother, but her husband's breath upon her neck was proving most distracting.

Sensing her discomfiture, her husband's arms tightened and as she squirmed she felt, rather than heard his deep, rumbling laugh against her. Giving up on the letter altogether, she sighed and turned to face her matrimonial match. She drew a deep breath but before she could speak, Sean kissed her lightly upon the cheek. Veronica smiled inwardly, marveling at the tenderness of her gentle giant. She gazed into his twinkling eyes, willing herself to look stern. "Dearest husband," she began with feigned reproach. "If you persist with such attention I'm afraid I'll never discover whether mother allowed Lucien to—"

A discreet cough announced the arrival of their butler, Ailbert. "I'm sorry to disturb ye, but a gentleman named Gordon Filsby is here to see ye," Ailbert said, looking abashed. He studiously gazed at a tapestry hanging across the room, giving the young couple a moment to compose themselves.

"Who is this Gordon? " Sean asked, recovering from the intrusion quickly. He stood out of habit, and waited for his servant to respond.

Ailbert looked up at Sean, then darted a quick look at Veronica before looking again at his employer of countless years. Before Ailbert could answer, Veronica stood and placed a hand upon her husband's arm to draw his attention. "He is the caretaker at my orphanage in Cornwall," she said quietly.

"Ye didna tell me we'd be receiving visitors today," Sean responded.

Veronica looked at her husband, relieved to see curiosity rather than admonishment in his eyes. "It must be serious for him to travel here to see us," she said, her voice betraying her concern. "I was not expecting him, else I would certainly have told you. I would very much like to know what has brought him here," she said.

"Show him in," Sean said, turning his attention back to Ailbert. With a nod, Ailbert quickly exited the room to fetch their visitor. Sean pressed his hand comfortingly atop that of his wife, which still gripped his arm. They released their contact when they heard the butler's returning footsteps.

A man dressed in dusty travelling clothes followed Ailbert into the room.

Veronica knew by the look on his face that something was dreadfully wrong. Not waiting for Ailbert to make introductions, she said, "Gordon, it is a pleasure to see you again. Please allow me to introduce my husband, Lord Sean McDonald.

"Call me Sean," said Sean with a polite bow.

The caretaker bowed in turn, clutching his hat tightly between his hands. "It is a pleasure to make your acquaintance sir," Gordon said looking up at the big Scotsman.

"What business brings ye so far from home on this day?" Sean asked, getting right to the point.

"Sir—, and my lady, something awful has happened. My Minnie is dead," Gordon said with teary eyes. Veronica gasped, causing Sean to reach a steadying arm out to her.

Oblivious of her husband's concern, Veronica quickly crossed the floor to embrace the distraught man. "Minnie was Gordon's wife," Veronica explained to her husband. She knew Gordon had loved his wife deeply.

"Come and sit down," Veronica urged. Guiding the trembling man gently to a chair, she waited until Gordon was settled before seating herself in the chair next to him. Leaning forward, she held his hand and said, "Tell us what happened."

"One day, Minnie and two little girls, Abigail and Lilly, disappeared," Gordon began. "We searched everywhere but couldn't find them. Three days later, the little girls just appeared at the front door. They didn't know where they had been, only that some bad men had grabbed them. They said the man who had talked to Minnie had an ugly face."

"An ugly face?" Veronica repeated, not comprehending.

"A scar," Gordon said as he ran his finger down his right cheek.

Veronica's face paled, and she looked like she might faint. "Parnell," she whispered, her hand rising to her throat.

"That's what we thought," Gordon said, nodding.

"Who is Parnell?" Sean asked, alarmed at his wife's reaction.

"How do you know Minnie is dead?" Veronica asked, not hearing her husband's question.

Gordon was also too distraught to realize Sean had spoken. "The little ones said they saw ships, so I knew they had been taken to London. So, I went there and asked around. I heard that a woman's body had been found in the Thames. It was Minnie," he said, tears falling from his eyes and onto his lap.

"Oh, dear God. This is my fault," Veronica said, tears beginning to trickle down her face as well.

"No, my Lady. You gave us four years of happiness that we would not have gotten otherwise. You saved her, and she loved the children she cared for," Gordon said.

"Someone, please tell me what is happening!" Sean commanded. He strode across the room to Veronica's side. Bending down he gathered her up into his arms and held her as she cried.

"Ailbert, I need you to find Murray," Veronica said through her tears. Taking a long shuddering breath, she pulled back slightly, unable to break from the confines of her protective husband's arms, then wiped her face.

"Yes, miss," said Ailbert.

"Please forgive me Sean, I didn't mean to cause you concern. Do you recall me saying that I used to help people? That I'd help get them out of bad situations?" said Veronica.

"Aye, ye told me some of the stories," Sean said.

"Well, Amy, our cook, was one of those people. I arranged for her to be removed from the clutches of a man named Feagin Parnell."

"And I guess he is nae a good man," Sean said.

"He is the spawn of the devil himself," Gordon said forgetting himself for an instant.

"My Lady, you needed to speak to me?" Murray interrupted as he entered the room.

"Yes, please come in," said Veronica. Sean released her so that she could again be seated.

Seeing the other man, Gordon stood and walked up to him.

"Good to see you, Gordon," Murray said as the two men shook hands.

"You also," said Gordon, managing a slight smile.

"What's happening?" Murray asked, seeing Gordon's and then Veronica's red eyes.

"Minnie has been murdered," Veronica said in a shaky voice. At the sound of a gasp, everyone turned to find Amy standing frozen at the door.

"Forgive me for intruding... I needed to speak to Murray, and I was told he was here," Amy said. "I couldn't help but hear... Minnie... how did Minnie die?" She asked. She wrapped her arms around herself as though suddenly feeling chilled.

"It's okay Amy, please come in," said Veronica. She stood and walked over to take a seat on the sofa. Sean remained where he was, but watched his wife cross the room with concern. Veronica patted the sofa, beckoning Amy to sit next her. "We believe Parnell found the orphanage and took Minnie and two little girls," she said once the other woman was seated.

"How do you know that?" Murray asked.

"The two girls were returned, and they described a man with a scarred face," Gordon explained.

"Why would a man like that return the lasses?" Sean asked.

"From what I know, Parnell doesn't deal in children, but it doesn't make sense for him to return them," Veronica said.

The sound of men's voices could be heard down the hall, on the other side of the door. The voices grew louder as the men got closer. Finally, Ian and Michael entered the room, halting their conversation abruptly when they noticed everyone standing around looking grave.

"What's wrong?" Ian asked.

"We believe Parnell found the orphanage in Cornwall and absconded with Minnie and two little girls. Minnie was murdered and found in the Thames. The girls were returned," Veronica said, summarizing what had happened.

Ian and Michael exchanged a grim look.

"What is it?" Veronica asked.

"There were two men in town asking questions about you. They were offering quite a bit of coin for information. That's what we came to tell you," said Michael.

"He knows it was me," Veronica said, growing pale.

"Would Minnie have—?" Amy began tentatively.

"Absolutely not. Minnie would not have betrayed you," Gordon retorted, not letting her finish the question.

"She didn't," Veronica said placatingly, looking at Gordon. She walked up to him and rested one hand on his arm. "She would have done what I instructed her to do. I told her that the children were to be protected no matter what," she said.

"But why would he return them?" Ian asked.

"A few of Parnell's men served with us on the Royal Anne. If Minnie made Parnell swear in front of his men, then he would have had no choice," Murray said.

"And now people in town are asking about you. Do you think that monster will send more men to try and hurt you?" Gordon asked, looking at Veronica with concern.

"He cannae trouble us here," Sean said, looking confident. "It's too secure, and the people would be up in arms if they got sae much as a hint that anyone meant to harm ye," he added.

"He will wait until you return to London to strike," Murray said to Veronica, avoiding Sean's eyes. He knew Sean would want to protect his wife, but felt it was important she realize she could not take this threat lightly.

"Do you really think he will wait for her to leave the castle?" Ian asked. Murray nodded. "But he can't know when that will be," Ian said.

"Parnell is a very patient man, and he will have people watching. He will wait until he knows he has the chance to take you," Murray said.

"We must assume he already knows I plan on going to London in a couple of weeks for Ada's wedding," Veronica said.

"No, ye won't go. If this man is as dangerous as everyone says, ye are safer here," Sean said. He noted the set of his wife's chin with dismay. Veronica did not cower in the face of danger, nor did she take well to being told what to do—not even by her husband. He shook his head both in frustration and begrudging admiration, knowing before she responded that she would not sit idle.

Veronica was quiet for a moment. "We will send a decoy," she finally said, nodding to herself. "My carriage will leave as planned. However, we will leave earlier, sneaking out under the cover of darkness. Gordon I need you to return to the orphanage and keep vigilant. Make sure all the little ones are safe."

"The carriage will carry someone pretending to be you, and it will be followed by several armed men. If they try anything, we will capture them. You will already be safe at your father's home before any of that happens," said Ian, working out the next steps of the plan.

"Then what?" Sean asked.

"Then we plan to stop Parnell for good," Veronica said.

* * *

A couple of days later, two men entered a room looking for Feagin Parnell. They found him talking to a couple of men.

"Gregory, Peter, you are back sooner than expected," Parnell said.

"Yeah, we were run out of town when we started asking questions about Veronica Aldridge," said the man called Gregory.

"So, you learned nothing?" Parnell asked from behind his desk.

"We learned a lot. The people there are very loyal and protective of her. But we did find one man who was willing to talk. We found out where she lived—which is in a castle by the way. It's a stronghold that we won't be able to infiltrate. It also seems she recently remarried to some highland lord's grandson."

"What Highland Laird?" asked one of his men with a strong Scottish brogue.

"McDonald," Gregory answered.

The man's face paled, and he looked at Parnell with wide eyes.

"We cannae touch that man. Laird McDonald is a powerful and mean bastard. If we harm a hair on his grandson's head, he will demand that England turn us over to him. I'd rather my head be stuck on a pike than be in Laird McDonald's hands."

"I have no discord with the man she married. So don't worry," Parnell said, waving his hand dismissively.

"You said she lives in a castle. Is there is no way we can reach her there, not even when she goes to town?" asked Maurice.

"The people there protect her. She is some sort of royalty to them."

"Do ye ken the castle's name?" asked the Scotsman.

"Do you remember what he called it?" Gregory asked, looking at Peter.

"Blackthorn," Peter replied.

The Scotsman closed his eyes and took a deep breath.

"Does that mean something to you?" Parnell asked.

"The lass is not some royalty. She is the direct descendant of Scotland royalty," said the Scotsman.

"How do you know that?" Parnell asked.

"Castle Blackthorn. Only a direct descendant inherits that place. If ye try to get to the lass there, ye are in for a fight," answered the Scotsman.

"So, we wait for her to come to England. We won't have to wait too long. I got word that an old friend is getting married, and Veronica Aldridge was invited to the wedding," said Parnell.

Gregory looked confused. Whom could Parnell be friends with on the same level as Veronica Aldridge?

"Anthony Carlyle," said Parnell, answering Gregory's unspoken question. He looked at Gregory with an evil glint in his eyes.

Gregory had known he'd need to do something, but had been unsure of what until that moment.

* * *

Two nights later, Randolph sat in a tavern at the docks. A woman approached his table, and sat down beside him.

"This had better be worth me coming out at this ungodly hour, Maives," Randolph said with a growl.

"Oh, it is, my lord," she said. Randolph loved hearing his employees refer to him as Lord.

"One of my regulars got too much into his cup and started blathering about a plan. His boss plans to capture the Marquess daughter," she said in a low voice. She looked around to make sure nobody overheard her.

"What did you say?" asked Randolph. She now had his full attention.

"They are planning on grabbing the Marquess daughter. What was her name?" Maives said, trying to remember.

"It wouldn't be Veronica, would it?" Randolph asked.

"Yes, that's it," answered Maives.

"This regular of yours... who does he work for?" Randolph asked.

"Parnell," Maives responded.

Randolph was shocked that Parnell would go after someone so dangerous. Henry would burn down the entire town to get to the person who hurt his daughter. *I merely mentioned her name, and the bastard wreaked havoc with my finances*, thought Randolph.

"My man said she did something that made Parnell angry, and he wanted to punish her. She is coming to London to go to a high falutin' wedding," said Maives.

Ada's wedding, thought Randolph. He began to wonder how he could take advantage of this situation. Reaching into his pocket, he pulled out a small bag of coins. He tossed the bag at Maives; she quickly grabbed it and held it to her chest.

"Thank you, my lord," she said.

"You earned it," he said as he got up and left the establishment.

* * *

Anthony lay in bed tossing and turning. He couldn't believe that just one week of having Ada in his arms had him missing her in bed. Despite the inconvenience of having to rise early to leave before the less discrete servants got wind of his visits, he had gotten used to the feel of her curled up against him. Getting up, he decided a drink might help him get to sleep. As he walked into his office, the hairs on his neck stood up, and he knew someone was there. Turning around, he saw the silhouette of someone sitting in the chair across from his desk.

"Whoever you are, breaking into my house was not a wise decision," Anthony said in a low, menacing voice.

"Captain, it's just me, Gregory," said the man as he stood with his hands up.

Anthony walked over to his desk, lit an oil lamp, then turned toward the man. "Gregory, what are you doing here?" He asked.

"I'm sorry for coming here, but I didn't know who else to turn to for help," said Gregory.

"I don't know why you came to me. After the lot of you went to work for Feagin, I washed my hands of you," said Anthony with a sigh. He walked over to a cabinet in one corner of the room and opened it. Uncorking a bottle of port, he poured two glasses, then walked over to Gregory and handed one to him.

"I know, sir, and if this weren't important, I would never have bothered you," said Gregory.

"Well, go ahead since you already went to the trouble of breaking into my home," said Anthony drily.

"Feagin plans to abduct and kill Lord Aldridge's daughter," Gregory said bluntly. He then downed his glass of port in one gulp.

Anthony stood frozen, unsure whether his ears were deceiving him. "Repeat that," he said.

Gregory told Anthony the story of Veronica dressing up as a boy and escaping with Amy, and of how Feagin found out. Anthony was shocked.

"He sent another man and me to Scotland to find her. We found out where she lives, but we told him there is no way for him to reach her there. Not only does she live in a castle, but the people there are very loyal to her. We found out she is a descendant of Scottish royalty, but that's not the most surprising thing we discovered. While we were watching the castle, I spotted Murray. He must have gone to work for her," said Gregory.

"So Murray betrayed Feagin. That was very brave," Anthony mused.

"Brave or stupid. If he finds out Murray's not dead, Feagin will make it his mission to make him so," said Gregory.

"When is he planning to get to Veronica?" Asked Anthony.

"When she comes to London for a wedding," Gregory answered.

Anthony's eyes grew wide. "That's my wedding," he said.

"Yes," said Gregory, nodding grimly.

"Do you have any details about what he plans to do?" Anthony asked.

"Not much. I know he is waiting to get more information about the wedding. He wants to know where it will be and if there will a ball afterward. He will tell us when he's decided what he wants to do," answered Gregory.

"Okay. I need you to get back. I don't want Feagin to notice you are missing. When you hear any more of his plans, come to me. I can't tell you how much I appreciate you coming here tonight," said Anthony.

"I know you tried to warn us about him. I wish I had listened to you and not believed his lies. But unfortunately, by the time we realized Feagin's plans, it was too late. We were already in too deep to get out. I'm sorry," said Gregory as he lowered his head.

"You help me stop Feagin, and I promise I will get you out of that life," Anthony said. He held his hand out to Gregory, who looked up and took it as if it were a lifeline.

"I will find out everything I can," Gregory said. Then he left the room without making a sound.

Anthony thought back to his days as captain of the Royal Anne. One of England's largest ships. He had trusted all of his crew—with the exception of the man who called himself Feagin Parnell. When the time came for Anthony and his crew to return home, Feagin convinced several of the other men to go work for him. He had boasted of big plans to purchase a fleet of ships, and had sold the other men on the dream of becoming rich quick. Anthony had known Parnell was not who he claimed to be. He'd tried to tell the others, but his concerns had fallen on deaf ears. He liked Gregory and was thankful he had come to him with Parnell's foolish plan. Now Anthony needed to speak with Thomas, to decide how best to proceed. He wrote a note, then went to wake up his footman. While he hated disturbing the man at such an early hour, this couldn't wait.

"Morris, wake up," Anthony called through the door when he reached the footman's sleeping quarters. Not hearing any response, he opened the door and entered the room. "Morris, I need your assistance," he said, but the man continued to snore lightly. He shook the man gently, and stood back when he finally opened his eyes.

"Sir?' Asked the footman, startled.

"I apologize for waking you, but I need you to deliver a message for me," said Anthony. The man rose quickly and got dressed without complaining.

Once the footman was gone, Anthony returned to his own bedroom. There was no more hope of sleep, but it didn't matter. The sun would be up in a couple of hours, and he couldn't stop thinking about Parnell. It was time for Anthony to delve into Parnell's past to discover just who he was dealing with.

Chapter Eight

"What's this about?" Callum Pearce asked when he walked into Thomas's office and saw Henry and Archie there.

"We will find out as soon as Anthony arrives. Please have a seat," Thomas said.

"It's good to see you, Archie," Callum said, seating himself next to Henry. Archie gave him a warm smile, and nodded in return.

"Do you think this meeting has something to do with Randolph?" Thomas asked.

"I really don't know. I thought that scoundrel would have made a move by now, but nothing has happened," Henry said. "Ah, right on time," he said when the butler entered the room to announce Anthony's arrival.

When Anthony walked into the office, he nodded to each of the men seated around the desk.

"Anthony, I believe you know everyone," Thomas said as he stood.

"Yes, Lord Pierce, Lord Corbin, Lord Aldridge," he said, looking once more at each of the other men.

"What is this about? When I received your cryptic message this morning telling me to gather everyone I trusted with my life, I must admit I feared the worst," Thomas said.

"Is this about Randolph?" Henry asked.

"No, I'm afraid a new problem has arisen. This is about Feagin Parnell. He is after your daughter." Anthony allowed the other men to absorb what he had said, noting the stunned look on each of their faces.

"Who is Feagin Parnell, and why is he after my daughter?" Henry asked, getting to his feet.

"I think we all should get comfortable. This might take a while," Anthony said. Heeding his advice, Thomas called to his butler, requesting that the furniture be rearranged to allow for a more relaxed conversation. When the butler and the servants who had helped him rearrange the sofa and chairs departed, Anthony recounted what Gregory had told him earlier that morning.

"If it were anybody other than Veronica, I would say hogwash. But knowing her as well as I do, I have a feeling it is true," Archie said as he looked at Henry.

"Yes, I'm afraid it is true. I myself didn't find out about it until Veronica was pregnant. She swore she was done rescuing people," Henry said.

"I knew that child was fearless, but to dress as a boy and go out into the night. That was foolish," Callum said.

"And now Parnell is after her," Henry said, closing his eyes.

"What are we going to do?" Thomas asked.

"Gregory is going to inform me when Parnell has finalized his plan. Let us wait until I have more information before deciding anything," said Anthony.

* * *

Around the back of Thomas's house, Aaron walked up to William, who was watching Ada and Meredith in the garden.

"What are you doing here?" William asked.

"I got a letter from Ian," Aaron said as he handed it to William. He waited in silence as the other guard read its contents.

"What do you think is going on?" William asked after reading the letter.

"I don't know. I was going to ask Henry, but he left early this morning, and didn't tell anyone where he was going," Aaron answered.

"He's here. So is Lord Pierce and Lord Corbin," said William.

"I don't think this is a coincidence," Aaron said. When William handed the letter back to him, he studied it, turning it over in his hands as though looking for something he missed.

"You must go in there now and tell them about this," said William. He raised a hand as Aaron turned to leave. "Go through the front door. We don't want to scare the women," he said, jerking his head in Ada and Meredith's direction. Aaron nodded, then headed towards the front of the house.

"What is it Walter?" Thomas asked with barely concealed irritation when his butler again entered the room. The men had been in the midst of discussing how best to get word to Veronica, and debating whether she should come to England or stay in Scotland.

"Excuse me, My Lord, but Lord Aldridge's man is here, and he says it's imperative he speaks with all of you immediately," the butler said.

"Show him in," Thomas said. Henry rose and walked over to meet Aaron.

"Excuse the intrusion, but I received word from Ian," Aaron said as he handed to letter to Henry.

As Henry skimmed the message, a look of puzzlement came over his face. He read it aloud for the others. "The beautiful birds are flying early this year. Even late at night, you can hear them. The first flock is not the one for watching. The important sighting will come later," he said. He looked at Aaron. "What does this mean?" He asked.

"It's code, sir." Aaron answered.

Intrigued, Anthony walked over to Thomas and took the letter from him, then read it through. "They are coming in early and at night. They have also sent a decoy," He said, then cocked his head thoughtfully. "Something is wrong for him to send a coded message," he said.

"Could she know?" Thomas asked.

"It's the only explanation for changing plans and using the cover of night, especially using a decoy. She will be coming in on horseback. It will be faster and quieter," Anthony said.

"How could she already know Parnell is after her?" Henry asked.

"Parnell? Feagin Parnell?" Aaron asked, looking at Anthony.

"We had better catch you up," Anthony said.

Anthony led Aaron back over to the couch, and once they were settled, he quickly recounted everything.

"Veronica will go to Owen's," Henry said.

"Why Owen's?" Anthony asked.

"She will want to get Leah to safety," Henry answered.

"Leah! Surely Veronica won't make that journey on horseback with Leah," Callum said.

"Veronica won't leave her behind with a threat like Parnell around," Henry said.

"You're right. We need to inform Owen so that he will be watching for their arrival," Callum said.

"Once they arrive, we will be able to form a plan. But, for now, Lord Pierce, you need to see Owen," said Anthony. He looked around the room then, making eye contact with each of the others. "I suggest all of you inform your families—and only your families—what is going on. We all must act normal but take extra caution. If Parnell is as intelligent as I think he is, he will be gathering information on everyone in Veronica's life," he said grimly. He let his words sink in for a moment before continuing. Then he said, "As soon as I learn more about what he intends to do, I will send word to Lord Claridge. He in turn will get word to each of you and will arrange a safe place for us to meet. For now, don't trust anybody, not even your staff. We don't know whether Parnell has eyes and ears in our homes."

"You are correct, Anthony. Right now, I need a level head to do my thinking. But, when it comes to my children, I tend to act first and think later," said Henry.

"As soon as you get word that Veronica has arrived safely, please inform Lord Claridge. I am sure it won't take long for Parnell to learn the details my wedding and devise a plan," Anthony said as he stood. "We should leave separately in case anyone is watching this house. I'd suggest waiting a few moments between each departure. As I said, Parnell could have spies anywhere," he said before leaving.

The others were quiet for a few minutes, as they processed what they'd learned. "Do you want William and me back at the house?" Aaron asked, breaking the silence.

"No. You two need to keep guarding Ada. In fact, if Parnell plans to grab Veronica at Ada's wedding, being here will put you both in the perfect position. Nobody will think twice about you being around," said Henry. Aaron nodded as he left the room. Thomas let out his breath, looking relieved that the guards would be staying at the house.

"I need to get going," Callum said as he stood. "I have a meeting with Owen," he added.

A few minutes later, Archie left, leaving only Henry and Thomas. "Did you ever imagine they would be so much trouble when we had daughters?" Thomas asked.

Henry chuckled. "No. I have to admit Veronica has been my biggest worry, but having something like this happen never crossed my mind."

"Even with everything that has happened, Ada is still my world. She will always be my little girl," said Thomas with a smile.

* * *

Two nights later, four people on horseback rode behind a house on Broads Street. Two men came out of a shed situated behind the house when they heard the horses approach. This caused the riders to stop quickly.

"Lady Veronica?" asked one of the men.

"Who wants to know?" Sean asked fiercely, looking down at the man from his horse.

Another rider lifted back the hood of their cloak, revealing a woman's face. "Charlie?" the woman asked.

The two men on the ground exchanged a look of relief. "Yes, my Lady. We were told to be expecting you," said the man Veronica had called Charlie. The two men stepped forward and took the reins of each of the horses as the riders dismounted.

Veronica pulled her cloak back to reveal her sleeping baby. She and Sean had fashioned a cloth around her so that Leah would be snuggled and secure against her chest while she rode. Sean walked over and held out his hands to take Leah from her. Once she'd handed the little girl to Sean, Veronica dismounted.

"It's good to see you again, My Lady," Charlie said, leading the four riders to the back door of the house. The other man led the horses into the shed.

"It's good to see you also," Veronica said with a kindly smile. When they reached the door, Charlie stood up straighter and rapped several times in quick succession. His knock and stance made Veronica think of someone seeking entrance to some secret club. She put her hand over her mouth to cover her smile.

When the door opened, Veronica recognized her old butler, Elliot, and his wife Claire behind him. When she spotted Claire, she immediately stepped forward, causing Elliot to take several steps back to make way for her. Paying no heed to her butler's awkwardness, she rushed to Claire and hugged her tightly.

"How has Owen been treating everyone?" Veronica said as she and Claire walked down the hall arm in arm. In her excitement, she momentarily forgot about the others, who followed a few steps behind.

"Very good. You left us in excellent hands. Elliot, you need to inform Lord Pierce that they have arrived," Claire said turning back to look at her husband with a smile.

Elliot bowed his head in acquiescence before departing, while Claire led the others into the drawing room to wait. When everyone was seated, she left to check on arrangements for their guests.

The travelers did not have to wait long before Owen appeared. He entered the room, and immediately looked around, as though searching for something. His eyes settled on Leah, who was sleeping in Sean's arms. A look of jealously flashed across his face.

Seeing his daughter in Sean's arms surprised Owen, causing his composure to slip briefly. He supposed it was only to be expected, since he and Veronica were no longer together. Forcing himself to ignore the stabbing pangs of envy, he arranged his expression into one of pleasant neutrality. He liked Sean, and knew the other man genuinely loved Leah. It gave him peace to know his daughter was safe and well cared for. Owen walked over to Sean, who carefully placed Leah in his arms. The baby stirred a little but immediately fell back to sleep.

"You were expecting us," Veronica said, more as a statement than a question.

"Yes. Father stopped by the other day and informed me you would be arriving sometime soon, and that it would be in the middle of the night," said Owen.

"How did he know I would come here and not somewhere else?" Veronica asked.

"They figured you would want to get Leah to safety first."

"I am not sure I understand. Ian sent word that we were coming in the night, but why would anyone think I needed to get Leah to safety? And who do you mean by 'they'?" Veronica asked.

Owen described the clandestine meeting his father and the others had attended at Lord Claridge's townhouse. He relayed everything his father had told him, adding, "We all know Feagin Parnell is coming for you."

Veronica looked around the room with wide eyes.

"How?" Ian asked.

"We can discuss this further tomorrow. It's late, and you all need to get some rest. You look tired," Owen said as he looked at Veronica. "I will send word of your safe arrival to your father. Don't worry about Leah tonight. I am quite happy to keep her with me. Sleep for as long as you wish," he added before leaving the room with Leah in his arms.

"He's furious with me," Veronica said once she knew Owen was out of earshot.

"Why do ye think that?" Sean asked. He moved closer to her, then wrapped his arms around her.

"I can tell. I have put our daughter in danger. I would be mad too if the situation were reversed," Veronica answered. "The sooner we catch Parnell, the sooner everything can go back to normal," she said.

Before Sean could respond, Claire returned and announced, "Your rooms are ready."

"Is everyone still working here?" Veronica asked as they walked up the stairs.

"Yes, although Lord Pierce did hire a new footman last week," Claire answered.

The others exchanged looks of concern. The timing of the new hire might not be coincidence.

"Show us his room," Ian said.

"This way," said Claire, realizing something was amiss. The group moved quickly down the corridor to the servant's quarters, careful not to make any undue noise. Claire pointed when she neared the new footman's quarters, moving aside to let Ian and Michael pass. The two men approached the door quietly; both leaned in close and pressed an ear to the door to determine whether there was someone within.

Suddenly, Ian and Michael took off running down the corridor, headed downstairs towards the back door. Veronica and Sean followed a few steps behind, with Claire trailing behind them. Veronica and Sean stepped outside in time to a man who had just climbed out one of the second-floor windows drop to the ground, only to be tackled by Ian and Michael.

"You have to let me go," the man begged.

"No, we don't," Ian said. He and Michael marched the man back upstairs, ignoring the man's pleas to be released. Only when they entered to the new footman's room did they let go of him. They pushed him roughly, causing the frightened man to sit clumsily on the bed.

When Veronica and Sean entered the room they came to stand beside Ian and Michael. Veronica looked at the stern faces of her companions and let out a breath of exasperation. She knew they meant only to protect her, but sometimes this aggravated her. Laying one hand on Sean's arm, she silently asked him to allow her to speak first. He looked at her with a raised eyebrow, but nodded his assent then signaled to Ian and Michael that she wished to speak.

Veronica looked at the seated man, surprised by how very young he looked. *He couldn't be more than fifteen*, she thought. "Did Parnell send you?" she asked in a not unkind voice.

"Yes," the young man said, looking at her nervously.

"What's your name?' Veronica asked.

"Arthur," he responded.

"What were your orders?" Ian asked, unable to remain quiet any longer.

"I was only to watch and see if a woman showed up," said Arthur.

"That's it? Just watch?" Ian asked.

"Yes. Well, that and also notify him as soon as she showed up," Arthur added.

"Do you know who I am?" Veronica asked.

"No. Parnell never gave me any names. He said I was to be hired here and was just to keep watch," Arthur said.

"My name is Veronica McDonald. I used to be Veronica Aldridge... as in Lord Henry Aldridge, the Marquees of Cambridge's daughter," Veronica said. She waited for Arthur to process what she had said. She did not have to wait long.

Arthur's eyes widened, then he lowered his head into his hands. When he raised it again, he looked at Veronica with tears in his eyes.

"I didn't know. I-I meant no harm. I was just doing what I was told. You have to let me go. Please," he said beseechingly.

"Why should we let you go?" Ian demanded.

"He knows where my parents live... He's a dangerous man, and if I don't do what he says..."Arthur said, his voice trailing off.

"How long have you worked for Parnell?" Veronica asked.

"Not long. I was working at the docks unloading ships. The man I worked for was taken to prison, and a man came and asked me and some of the other fellows if we needed work. My family only has me to take care of them, so I couldn't say no," Arthur said, looking down at the floor.

Veronica walked over to the far side of the room and took hold of a chair that was situated in the corner. She dragged it, brushing off Sean's attempts to help, and positioned it directly in front of Arthur, then seated herself upon it. She stared at Arthur, waiting for him to look up. When he did, she said, "We are going to let you go, but you must agree to go to Parnell and tell him the truth. Tell him that a woman arrived, but she showed up during the day, not in the dead of night. You can say you waited until nightfall before sneaking out of the window to come see him. That way, you are mostly telling the truth, and he won't suspect anything."

"What are ye thinking?" Sean asked.

"We can't hide. Parnell will know sooner or later that I am here, and Arthur needs to take care of his family," Veronica said simply. She looked at Sean, hoping he would see her logic.

"Thank you, my Lady," Arthur said gratefully.

"Remember Arthur, that is all you are going to tell him. Parnell wants me dead, and we know the man is planning something. It would be best if you remain aware of things around you. You must do what he tells you but try to avoid trouble. One day Parnell will be dealt with, and it would not be advisable for you to be associated with his endeavors."

"I will do exactly as you say, my lady. And if I can repay your kindness, I will," he said with conviction.

"I believe you. Parnell will send you back here so you can keep feeding him information. Please do come back. We will keep your involvement in this situation a secret so you need not fear any recrimination," Veronica said as she stood and moved out of Arthur's way.

"Leave out the window. You want to make your escape look real," Ian said. Arthur bolted towards the window immediately, causing Ian to smile.

Halfway out the window, Arthur looked back at Veronica, then nodded before disappearing out of sight.

"I hope we did the right thing," Ian said.

"I might be wrong, but I think we now have someone on the inside," said Michael.

"I hope so. We are going to need all the help we can get," said Veronica, as she turned to toward the door. Suppressing a yawn, she added, "Now, let's go to bed, and a good night to all."

Chapter Nine

Owen awakened to the feel of little Leah kicking his back. Rolling over, he discovered she had turned sideways and was steadily kicking her legs. "I'm awake," he said, laughing at her antics. He played with her for a while, marveling at how much more active she was since the last time he'd seen her.

"You woke up in a good mood. Let's get you cleaned up and dressed," he finally said, noticing she was wet.

Sitting Leah on the floor, he knelt down to dig through her satchel, finding clothes and napkins. Necessary items assembled, he then turned to pick her up, only to realize she was gone.

"Leah, where did you go?" Owen asked. Scratching his head, he stood and looked around. Hearing her babbling, he walked around the sofa to discover her standing, holding onto a table.

"Look at you already standing up," he said, amazed. He swooped her up into his arms, causing her to giggle. As he lay her down on the bed and began to change her, she began babbling again.

"I have missed so much. Do you know how happy I am to wake up with you here?" He asked. Leah looked at him and smiled. Owen felt tears prick his eyes, and a sudden lump form in his throat. Picking his daughter up, he held her close, and kissed her forehead.

"Let's go get you something to eat," he said as they left his room.

* * *

Veronica and Sean came down the stairs around ten o'clock that morning. Entering the drawing room, they found Owen on the floor, playing with Leah. Veronica's heart warmed as she watched Owen play with his daughter.

"Did you sleep well?" Owen asked when he noticed them.

"Yes. I didn't realize how tired we were," Veronica said. She walked over and knelt to kiss her daughter on the forehead.

"Ma-ma," said Leah, reaching for Veronica. Smiling, Veronica picked her up and went to sit down, settling Leah on her lap.

"Did you have fun with your father?" Veronica asked.

"It felt good to wake up with her. I missed her so much," Owen said, sitting in the chair next to Veronica. He held his hand out, letting Leah play with his fingers. "I put her down to get her a change of clothes, and the next thing I knew, she was gone. I found her standing in front of the sofa," he said.

"By herself? She stood on her own?" Veronica asked, surprised.

"Yes," answered Owen.

"I missed her first time standing up by herself!" Veronica said, kissing Leah's forehead again.

Owen couldn't hide his smile. He was pleased he had gotten to see his daughter do something for the first time. Sean gave Veronica a questioning look. Leah had already been standing on her own for a month.

"I got to see you stand for the first time," Owen said, his voice full of emotion. He gently took Leah from Veronica and hugged her. Sean smiled as he realized what Veronica had just given Owen.

"I sent word to your father that you made it safely," Owen said.

"Ye need to tell him what happened last night," Sean said, looking at Veronica.

Owen looked over at Sean, who had seated himself on the sofa across from them.

"What happened last night?" Owen asked.

"The man you recently hired is one of Parnell's men," Veronica answered.

"Do you mean Arthur?" Owen asked. Veronica nodded her head. "Where is he now?" he asked.

"We had a word with him and let him go to inform Parnell that I had arrived. I don't know if he will return, but if he does, he will need to stay here and work as normal," Veronica said.

"What? Someone explain what happened and why I would keep him in this house?" Owen said, shocked.

"First, tell me how you knew we were coming here, and that Parnell is after me?" Veronica said.

"I think this is going to take a while. Why don't we get you both something to eat. You missed breakfast, so I told Claire to have lunch made early. I will tell you everything then," Owen said as he stood, still holding Leah firmly in his arms.

* * *

After lunch, they returned to the drawing room. Veronica called for Ian and Michael to join them.

"Michael, I will need you to stay here today," Veronica said. Michael looked surprised.

"But I should be with you in case something happens," he said in protest.

"If Parnell sees he cannot get to me directly, he will find another way," Veronica said. She gathered Leah into her arms and walked over to Michael. He looks down at Leah fondly, smiling as she reached out to grasp one of his outstretched hands. He wiggled his fingers playfully, causing Leah looks up at him and laugh. Michael loved children, and treated Leah like she were his own.

"I understand. I will protect her with my life," Michael said, directing his gaze from Leah to Veronica.

Veronica moved over to stand with Sean, who wrapped his arm around her supportively. He knew it would be difficult for his wife to leave Leah, regardless of how well protected she might be. "She is eating mostly from the table now, so she should be fine without me. I will return as soon as I can. It may be difficult as I know my father will try to keep me under lock and key."

"It would appear suspicious if you did not come back to be with your daughter," Owen said.

"You're right. That will be an excellent argument for my father; perhaps it will convince him to relinquish some of his protectiveness."

"I will go arrange for our things to be brought out. Ye spend this time with the wee lass," Sean said. He bent down to kiss Veronica's forehead, then Leah's, before leaving the room.

"I will not let her out of my sight," Owen said after Sean left. He walked up to Leah and touched her head.

"Did Arthur return last night?" Veronica asked, looking at Ian.

"Yes," said Ian.

"Go get him," Owen said with an uncharacteristic snarl in his voice. Ian looked at Veronica, who nodded her head.

"Owen, you must not lose your temper. He is a young man who was just trying to take care of his parents. Everyone makes mistakes. I think Arthur genuinely regrets his decision to help Parnell," said Veronica.

Owen looked away so that Veronica could not read his face. He thought about his own misdeeds and the pain his actions had caused for so many people. Before he could reply, Ian returned. Arthur followed a few steps behind, his hat in his hand, with eyes downcast.

"Arthur, we have informed Lord Pierce of your employment arrangement with Parnell. Please tell us what his most recent his orders were," Veronica said.

"He said I am to continue to watch and listen to what goes on in the house. And he wants to know if I hear anything about you attending a wedding," Arthur said, not looking up.

Owen and Veronica exchanged a knowing look. "He is going to do it at the wedding," Owen said. Veronica nodded.

"Of course. It will be crowded, especially at the celebration following the ceremony. It will be easy for one of his men to slip in unnoticed," Veronica said.

Veronica turned her attention back to Arthur, moving closer to him. As she approached, Arthur slowly lifted his head. He looked at Veronica, and then at the child she held in her arms. Leah gazed up at Arthur and smiled. Arthur could not help but smile back, enchanted.

"This is Leah. She is my child by Lord Pierce. I know you must consider the safety of your parents, but please consider this innocent baby as well. I hope that if you hear Parnell say anything about harming or absconding with her, you will let Lord Pierce know immediately."

Arthur looked at Leah, then back a Veronica as he contemplated her words. "I swear on my life and everything holy. If I hear anything from Parnell about this beautiful little girl, I will go straight to Lord Pierce," he said.

"Thank you, Arthur," said Veronica.

"No, thank you, my Lady—for your forgiveness and for placing your trust in me. You are too kind," Arthur said, gratitude shining in his eyes.

"You can go back to your duties," Owen said curtly. He had held his temper, but did not have Veronica's capacity for forgiveness. Arthur bowed quickly then and walked away.

"You're right. I need him here," Owen said when he knew Arthur was gone.

"Owen, Parnell is an evil man. There is nothing he won't do to get what he wants. I know Leah will be safe with you. If something should happen to me, please tell her how much I loved her, and that she was my life," Veronica said. Though her voice remained steady, tears ran down her face.

"Nothing is going to happen to you," Owen said fervently. He raised his hand and cupped her face, using his thumb to wipe away her tears.

"You cannot know that," Veronica said quietly.

"I do know that between your father and mine, and the help of their friends, they will come up with a plan. Of that I am sure. Parnell will not have a chance to get anywhere near you," Owen said. He kissed Veronica's forehead, ignoring the familiar stab of unrequited his love as he inhaled her scent.

* * *

When it was time to leave, Veronica was reluctant to let Leah go. "I love you," she whispered into Leah's ear one last time before handing her over to Owen. She looked over to where her carriage and Sean were waiting, conflicted.

"Come here, sweetheart," Owen said as he took Leah in his arms. To Veronica he said, "She will be safe here. I will be expecting you to return in a couple of days." He smiled reassuringly.

Veronica looked to Michael then. He nodded, letting her know he has everything under control. Veronica managed a half smile, then turned and left without looking back.

Once inside their carriage, she finally allowed herself to break down. Sean held her as she cried, softly rubbing her back, not saying anything. When she stopped crying, she sat up and wiped her face.

"I'm sorry for being so emotional," she said.

"It be all right. I am used to it by now," Sean said, teasingly. Veronica playfully slapped his arm, which caused him to laugh. Feigning injury, he held his arm, pretending to dodge her attack.

"I know I have been overly sensitive lately," she said, settling back against the seat.

"I love ye," Sean said. He reached for her gloved hand and brought it to his lips for a quick kiss.

"I love you too," she said, smiling at him.

* * *

Henry and Ellen were waiting for them when they reached her father's house. Veronica immediately ran to her father, who enfolded her in his arms and held her tight.

"My turn," Ellen said, smiling. She opened her arms, then drew Veronica in for a warm embrace.

"Let's go into the dayroom and talk," Henry said as he shook Sean's hand.

"Father, how does everyone know about Parnell?" Veronica asked, unable to wait any longer.

"A man who works for Parnell went to Lord Carlyle and told him what he was planning," Henry said.

"Lord Anthony Carlyle? The man Ada is marrying?" Veronica asked, surprised. Her father nodded. "Well, we believe that is where he plans to try and take me," she said.

"Yes, we are aware of that also," Ellen said.

"Start from the beginning. You need to tell us what has happened. How do you know about Parnell? And why did you decide to come in the middle of the night," Henry said.

Veronica told her parents everything. She began by telling them about Gordon's visit and Minnie's disappearance and death. She shared that Parnell's men had been in town asking questions about her, and how from that they'd figured out Parnell must have found out about her secret activities.

"Now we must wait until Anthony's contact gets back in touch with him. When we know what Parnell intends to do, we will devise a plan and stop him," Henry said. What he did not tell his daughter or Sean was that he was already developing a plan of his own that would remove the threat of Parnell for good.

"Aye, we will stop him," Sean said, holding Veronica's hand.

Veronica took a deep breath and smiled, first at Sean, and then her parents. She desperately wanted to share their confidence. But something inside told her it wasn't going to be that easy.

Chapter Ten

A week before the wedding, Anthony visited the Claridge home. Ada ran into his arms as soon as he entered the front door.

"I have missed you," she said.

"I have missed you too," Anthony responded. Anthony's business affairs, and the demands that planning such a large wedding had placed on Ada had prevented them from seeing each other as often as they would have liked.

"I wasn't expecting you," she said as she pulled back reluctantly. His arms remained loosely around her.

"I need to speak to your father, and it gave me an excuse to see you," Anthony said as he kissed her forehead.

When Ada smiled, Anthony could not stop himself from staring at her. He loved seeing the happiness in her eyes when she looked at him. He thought back to when he first saw her. He was so glad he had acted upon the instinct that told him she would make a fitting partner. She had proven to be the perfect match for him, and knowing she had fallen in love with him made his heart beat faster, even now. He hadn't said the words himself yet, but he believed he felt it inside.

"Anthony, so glad you made it. Ada, sweetheart, I must speak with Anthony alone," Thomas said when he came upon them.

"Yes, father," Ada replied, still looking at Anthony.

Anthony kissed her hand, then followed Thomas down the corridor that led to his office.

"What have you found out," Thomas asked as soon as the door was shut.

* * *

Ada had just returned to her bedroom when she remembered something Meredith said to her before she left to meet Ellen for tea. Meredith had wanted her to remind her father that she would be late returning. Turning on her heel she headed towards her father's study. She noticed one of their footmen standing outside the door, with his head leaned against it.

"Jones, what are you doing?" she asked, startling the man.

"I needed to speak to Lord Claridge, but I saw he was in a meeting and decided to wait," Jones responded quickly.

"He should be done momentarily. I will let him know you wish to speak to him," she said.

"Thank you, my Lady," Jones said, then bowed and walked away.

That was strange, thought Ada as she watched Jones depart. She turned to knock on the door but paused when she heard Anthony's voice.

"Gregory visited me last night. Parnell intends to get to Veronica during the wedding ball," said Anthony.

"At least we know when it will happen, " Thomas said.

"We must formulate a plan. Do you have a place for all of us to meet that won't look conspicuous?" Anthony asked.

There was a pause, then Ada heard her father say, "Meredith is taking Ada for the final fitting for her wedding dress and trousseau tomorrow. Ellen and Eleanor will accompany them, since Ada has asked them to be her attendants at the wedding. If we were to drop them at the dress shop, it would not seem amiss for us to wait for them across the street at Gordon's Tea room."

"Excellent," said Anthony in response.

Ada didn't know what to think about what she had just heard, but she resolved to be forthcoming. She knocked on the door, waiting to be invited in.

"Come in," said Thomas.

"Father, I am sorry to interrupt, but mother asked me to tell you she wouldn't be back until late this afternoon," Ada said. She looked down at the floor, not knowing how to tell them she had overheard their conversation.

"Ada, what's wrong?" Anthony asked. He knew Ada well enough by now to when she wanted to say something but was unsure how to bring it up.

"I'm sorry. I didn't mean to eavesdrop," Ada blurted.

"What did you hear?" Thomas asked, sounding aggravated.

"I was coming to tell you what mom had said, when I saw Jones standing outside your door."

"Wait a minute. Jones was standing outside the door?" Thomas asked.

"Yes, he said he needed to speak to you, but he knew you were in a meeting and had decided to wait," she said. She noticed Anthony and her father looking at each other strangely.

"I need to know what you heard and what part of our conversation Jones heard, "Anthony said as he walked up to Ada.

"Are you angry with me?" Ada asked, looking up at Anthony with tear-filled eyes. She still feared doing something that would cause him to change his mind about marrying her.

"No, Ada, I am not mad. On the contrary, I am delighted that you came in and were honest about listening to your father and I from the other side of the door. You must tell us what you heard," said Anthony.

"I heard you say someone was planning on taking Veronica at the ball," Ada said.

"Where was Jones when you heard this?" Anthony asked.

"He had already walked away by then," Ada answered.

Ada could see both her father and Anthony breath out heavily, visibly relaxing. "What's going on? Who is this person wanting to take Veronica?" she asked.

"Ada, you don't need to be involved," Thomas said firmly.

"No, father, I need to know what's happening," said Ada.

"Ada," Anthony said, turning her towards him. Ada looked up at him with defiance in her eyes. "I need your help. Can I trust you to help me?" Anthony asked as he held her forearms.

"Yes, you can trust me," she said, her jaw still tight.

"There is a threat to Veronica's life. I and your father and several others will ensure she is safe, but that means my time must be spent wisely. Marrying you is important to me, and I would be grateful if you would continue to manage the preparations. Can you make sure our nuptials are perfect? Can you do that for me?" Anthony asked.

"Yes, of course. I would do anything to help you," said Ada.

Anthony smiled and kissed her hand, looking into her eyes. "I also need you to act as if you never heard what was discussed here today. Can you do that?"

"Yes," she said, nodding her head and smiling.

"Good, now there are still some things your father and I must discuss. May I come find you before I leave?" Anthony asked. Ada nodded, then left the room.

When the door closed behind her, Thomas turned to Anthony, looking at him with surprise. "You have a way with her," he said.

"I understand that she wants to live a productive life again. She wants to feel wanted and needed," said Anthony.

Thomas thought about what Anthony said. He had to admit it made sense that Ada had felt unwanted and excluded from many aspects of her former daily life after what had happened. For months, she had been forced to watch out her window as life went on around her.

"How long has Jones worked for you?" Anthony asked.

"For at least six months. Long before this thing with Veronica came about. I didn't think any of my people could be working for him. I suppose you think I should remove him from my employment?" Thomas said as he wiped his forehead.

"No. I suggest you inform Aaron of your suspicions about Jones; he will keep an eye on him. Don't give Jones any reason to suspect you are on to him. Let this be a reminder that Parnell could have someone in each of our households. It matters not how long they have been employed with us. No one is above suspicion," said Anthony.

"I will suggest that everyone to be extra cautious when I give them the details of our next meeting," Thomas said.

"I would now like to spend some time with my soon-to-be bride," Anthony said, exchanging a smile with Thomas.

When Anthony left his office, Thomas sat down in his chair and laid his head back. He closed his eyes and thanked God for allowing Anthony to come into their lives. Opening his eyes again, he sat forward, then extracted a piece of paper from inside his desk. He paused briefly, thinking about what to write. It had to be something that would ensure everyone attended the meeting without giving anything away; this was especially important now that he knew he couldn't trust anyone in his household.

* * *

The next day, Anthony waited in his carriage, watching Ada and the other ladies enter the Modiste shop. Waiting a few extra moments, he then exited his carriage and walked into Gordon's tea shop. Once inside, he was directed to a private room, where he found the others waiting.

Henry and Thomas stood on the right side of the room with Lord Corbin and Lord Pierce. Anthony's eyes grew large when he spied a man the size of a mountain standing with them. *That must be Veronica's Scottish husband*, he thought. To his left, Veronica was seated at a table sipping tea. She appeared to be deep in thought as she studied her teacup, but she raised her head when she heard the door close behind him.

"Gentlemen and Lady," Anthony said, nodding his head to greet each of them.

"Anthony, what did your man say?" Henry asked, not wasting time on pleasantries.

"Parnell will attempt to… reach Lady Veronica at the wedding ball my father is hosting for Ada and me," Anthony began, glancing at Veronica. He chose his words carefully, not wishing to frighten her unduly. Her gaze was reassuringly steady as she looked back at him, so he continued. "As you all well know, my father is a pickthank. He has a predilection for extravagance, which will require him to hire more staff," he said.

"That means Parnell will be able to put more of his men into play," Lord Corbin said.

"That is what we thought as well. So, we will watch Veronica, and when Parnell's men make their move, we detain them and force them to confess," Henry said.

"No," Veronica said, standing up.

Everyone in the room turned to look at her, surprised by her objection. Veronica walked up to her father, maintaining eye contact with him. "We let them take me," she said.

"What?" Henry and Sean said at the same time.

"We will have to have the magistrate there to arrest Parnell. These men might be too afraid of him to talk," said Veronica.

"It's unsafe, lass. I cannae sae much as think of ye being in danger," Sean objected.

"I know you are all worried about me, but—" Veronica began.

"The answer is no. You are pregnant, and I will not put both you and your unborn child at risk," Henry said in a stern voice.

The other men in the room appeared shocked to learn she was with a child.

"I'm only a few months along. And it is all the more the reason why we should end this now. I cannot wait until I am round with child and unable to defend myself," Veronica said. She had moved to stand by Sean, and she now reached for his hand in silent support as she looked at her father.

"Father, you know I have no qualms about defending myself and I will do what I must. This is what must happen. We need to have a plan in place to ensure you can follow me to wherever Parnell may take me," she said.

"I don't want you in that situation ever again," Henry said, closing his eyes.

"My Lord's, please forgive my saying so, but she does have a point," Ian said. Anthony turned to see Ian standing in the corner. He hadn't even realized the man was there, he'd blended so well into his surroundings. It made Anthony appreciate how good the four men who worked for Henry really were.

"I'm sorry, gentlemen, but the Lady Veronica is correct. We must follow her to where she is taken if we are to capture Parnell. It would be folly to rely only on the hope that his men will be forthcoming with the information we require concerning Parnell's whereabouts," Anthony said.

"I don't like the idea of putting a woman in danger—especially one who is with child," Archie said.

"Neither do I, but it might be the only way," Thomas said with difficulty. Henry was quiet as he considered the options.

"Henry. What do you think?" Thomas asked him. Henry looked from face to face, seeing that they each saw the logic in what Veronica had proposed. He then turned to his daughter. "You are going to do this no matter what I say?" he asked.

"Yes, father. I dislike going against your wishes but this needs to be resolved. Neither Leah nor my unborn baby will be safe until Parnell is dealt with," Veronica said.

Henry stared at her for a few seconds, then smiled. "All right. Does anyone have a plan for how to keep track of my daughter?" He asked.

Anthony watched Henry; something inside told him Henry had agreed too quickly.

"My Lord, I believe I can help with that," Ian said.

"Then come and join us. Tell us what you shall do," Henry said. Ian drew closer, and began to explain his idea. The group spent the next hour going over the plan, working out the details. Henry was unusually quiet, nodding occasionally when it was required of him.

"Henry, do you mind staying for a while longer?" Anthony asked when the meeting concluded.

"Of course," Henry replied. He then turned to Veronica. "I will see you and Sean back at the house. I have requested that Owen attend supper with us this evening. I am eager to see my granddaughter," he said.

"Then expect Ann and me for dinner as well," Callum said, inserting himself into the conversation. He ignored the sour look on Henry's face.

"Yes, father," Veronica said with a wink at Callum. She then turned and curtsied to the men before leaving with Sean.

"My Lady," Anthony said, bowing slightly. After Veronica and Sean departed, the room cleared out rapidly.

"What did you want to discuss?" Henry asked Anthony once they were alone.

"What are you planning?" Anthony asked bluntly.

"Pertaining to what?" Asked Henry evasively.

"You're going to kill Parnell," Anthony stated, making it clear it was not as a question.

"Whatever would make you think that?" Henry asked, looking away.

"It's what I would do, if I were in your place. But I would ask you not to," said Anthony.

"Why not?" Henry asked, giving up on hiding his intention.

"Feagin Parnell is not whom he portrays to be," said Anthony.

"What are you saying?" Henry asked, not comprehending.

"There is more to the man than any of us know. Please just give me until the day before my wedding. If I discover nothing, then you are free to do what you will. I shall not stand in your way."

Henry was quiet for a moment as he stared at Anthony. "All right. You have until the day before your wedding. But know this. I will do what I must to protect my daughter," he said.

The two turned to leave, but suddenly Anthony stopped short. "If I may ask? What did Veronica mean when she said she had no qualms about protecting herself?" He asked.

"Let this go no further. Veronica once killed a man who was trying to harm her. I witnessed it myself. She was only sixteen." Henry said. He then told Anthony the story about her stabbing the man who had tried to kill her after she'd proven he had harmed another girl.

Anthony was shocked. There was so much more to Veronica than what met the eye. He wondered if she was someone he might be able to rely upon in the future.

* * *

Feagan sat behind his desk reviewing shipment documents when a knock sounded at the door. "Come in," he said gruffly.

"Sir, Malcolm Randolph wishes to speak to you," a voice on the other side of the door said.

Feagin looked up, surprised. "Let him in," he said. He had never had any dealings with Randolph, but he'd heard of him by reputation. It made him simultaneously curious and wary. As Randolph walked into the room, Feagin took the opportunity to look the man over. Dressed in expensive clothes, he walked with an air of importance; but it was his cane that garnered Feagin's attention. It was made of a black wood, embellished with what must have been silver. At the top of it was a carved bear's head, it's mouth open in a snarl.

"Please, sit. What brings you to see me?" Feagin asked, sitting back in his chair.

"I was hoping you could do something for me," Randolph said as he sat down.

"What is that?" Feagin asked, narrowing his eyes.

"When you abduct Veronica Aldridge, I want you to take Ada Claridge as well," said Randolph.

Feagin did not betray any reaction to Randolph's request. Not even a blink. He stared straight at the other man. "Why her?" He asked, realizing it would do no good to deny that was his plan to Randolph.

"Certain people think they can take what is mine," said Randolph.

"And this Ada is yours?" Feagin asked.

"Yes. She was to marry me before Carlyle stepped in the way," Randolph said, gritting his teeth.

Feagin sat very still, thinking. His eyes never left Randolph's face. "First, tell me how you heard about my plans for the Aldridge chit," he said.

"A man of yours visited one of my establishments. He was a little chatty whilst in bed," Randolph said with a smirk.

Rage engulfed Feagin, though his demeanor did not show it. "What establishment?" He asked calmly.

"The Pelican," answered Randolph.

"If you are indeed *asking* me to do this for you, it would imply I have the option of saying no. But I do not think you are asking," said Feagin.

"I don't know what Veronica Aldridge has done to incur your wrath, but I must warn you, the Marquess is not someone to be trifled with. He is not the sort of man to call you out for pistols at dawn. He will simply make you disappear. I merely made a casual comment about his daughter, and my financial endeavors suffered almost immediately because of it," said Randolph.

"Is there a chance Lord Aldridge would discover my plans if I refused your request?" Parnell asked, knowing the answer already. There was nothing to stop Randolph from going to Henry.

"There is always a chance. Just look at how easy it was for me to figure it out," Randolph said, staring at his cane as if he were growing bored with the conversation.

Feagin did not move, though he rapidly turned over Randolph's threat in his mind. This was a complication he did not need. He needed to appease Randolph to give himself time to figure things out. "All right. What's one more? I will send word when it's time to collect your prize," he said.

"Excellent. I will await word from you." Randolph said. He stood and dipped his head, then turned and left the room.

Feagin stood up and walked over to the bar beside the fireplace. He poured himself a drink and took a sip. With a snarl, he threw the glass and its unfinished contents into the fireplace, causing the flames to leap up temporarily. The door opened quickly.

"Sir, is everything all right?" said the man who'd come in.

"Come in Maurice, and close the door," Feagin said as he returned to his desk and sat down. "I need to know which of my men have been to the Pelican recently," he said.

"Several of us went there a few days ago," said Maurice.

"And whom all enjoyed a light skirt that night?" asked Feagin in a steely voice.

The man was quiet as he thought for a few seconds. "Clive and Rufus," he finally answered.

"They were the only ones?" Asked Feagin.

"Yes sir. May I ask what this is about?" Maurice said.

"Someone has betrayed me. Randolph knows my plans for the Aldridge girl and now thinks he can blackmail me into doing something for him," said Feagin. The other man's eyes widened.

"What is he wanting?" Maurice asked.

"He wants us to take Ada Claridge at the same time," answered Feagin.

"The bride you mean," Maurice said, looking at Feagin for confirmation. When Feagin nodded, he asked,. "Did he say how he knows?"

"One of our men informed his whore at the Pelican," said Feagin.

"It had to be Clive," said Maurice.

"What makes you think it was him?" Feagin asked.

"He was complaining that night. He said the plan was foolhardy, and that we would wind up getting killed for going against the Marquess," said Maurice.

Feagin was disappointed. He liked Clive, but this transgression could not be overlooked. "I need some time to think. Say nothing," he said to Maurice.

"I'll say nothing," Maurice repeated, before leaving the room. Feagin sat staring out a window going over everything in his head. His well-laid plans had been ruined, and now he has to deal with Randolph. The man was a fool, thinking he could blackmail him into getting what he wanted. It would cost him everything, Feagin thought as a smile crept across his face.

Chapter Eleven

The day before his wedding, Anthony was in his office dealing with some last-minute business. He wanted to get as much done as possible so that he and Ada could go away for a few days after the wedding. With everything that had been going on, he had completely forgotten this promise to Ada.

He had heard nothing from his man about Parnell, which meant there was no way he could stop Henry from killing the man. *It would be better if Parnell did disappear*, Anthony mused. In spite of this, he still believed Parnell was not to be underestimated. Looking up, he noticed his butler standing in the doorway.

"My Lord, Mr. Lathom is here to see you," his butler announced.

"Show him in," said Anthony.

Anthony stood up from behind his desk as the man entered the room. "Good to see you Lathom. Do you have news for me?" he asked.

"Yes. Something strange happened last night. Parnell left abruptly late in the night," said Lathom.

"What was strange about that?" Anthony asked.

"He left out a window. Clearly he didn't want his men to know he was leaving. I noticed him sneaking out so I followed him into a wealthy district. This is the address." Lathom said as he handed Anthony a piece of paper. He noticed the color drain from Anthony's face as he started at it. "My Lord, is everything all right?" He asked.

"Are you sure this is where Parnell went?" Anthony demanded.

"Yes," answered Lathom.

"Listen to me, Lathom. I want you to stop watching him. This is over. Stay away from Parnell," said Anthony. He strode over to one corner of the room, then bent down in front of a safe. Retrieving a leather pouch from the safe, he stood up, opening it as he walked back to Lathom. "Here is what I owe you, and a little extra. Are you sure he didn't see you?" He asked.

"Yes. I am sure," Lathom said, becoming nervous. He had never seen Anthony appear so shaken.

"To be safe, I want you to stay away for a few days," Anthony said.

"My Lord, what's troubling you?" Lathom asked.

"I cannot say as of now, but please trust me on this," answered Anthony.

"Yes, My Lord. I will," said Lathom.

Anthony relaxed and held out his hand. Lathom looked at it with surprise, then shook it. No one from the upper peerage had ever offered their hand to him before.

"If you ever need my services again, please don't hesitate to get in touch. I am your man," Lathom said with a bow.

"Thank you, Lathom. God be with you," said Anthony.

"And you, sir as well," Lathom said before leaving the office.

Anthony walked back to his desk and sat down. Putting his elbows on the desk, he held his head in his hands while he processed what he'd read. With a start, he lifted it again as he remembered something.

"Henry," he said, jumping up and running to the door.

"Walter!" He hollered to his butler.

"Yes, My Lord," answered Walter.

"Is my carriage ready?" Anthony asked.

"Yes, My Lord," said Walter.

"Bring it around," Anthony said as he ran up the stairs to finish getting ready. He prayed he would be able to catch Henry and stop him before things went very wrong.

* * *

Henry was in his office with Ian and William discussing their plan to eliminate Parnell, when a knock sounded at the door. "Come in," said Henry.

"My Lord, Lord Carlyle is here and says it is imperative that he speak with you," said his butler.

"Bring him," Henry said. He did not ask the men in his office to leave, knowing Anthony's unexpected visit must have something to do with Parnell.

Anthony looked serious as he entered the room. "Lord Henry," he said, nodding perfunctorily. Noticing Henry's men, he nodded again. "Gentlemen," he said.

"You can dispense with the niceties. I assume you have some new information," Henry said.

"Have you implemented your plan yet?" Anthony asked. He didn't use names because he wasn't sure who might be listening.

"No. We were just discussing that very thing," Henry said.

"You must stop. I have learned something that is detrimental to all of us. We must go through with the original plan to allow Veronica to be captured," said Anthony.

"Why? What is it that you know?" Henry asked.

Anthony walked to the door and opened it. He stuck his head outside and looked around. Satisfied no one was eavesdropping, he then closing the door and returned to stand near the other men. "Parnell is working for the Home Office," Anthony said in a low voice.

Henry looked at Anthony with wide eyes. Ian and William look at each other stunned. What could Parnell possibly be doing working for the British Government?

"Are you certain?" Henry asked.

"Yes. If you kill him or he disappears, there will be an inquiry. And if it surfaces that he went after a member of your family, then the attention will be on you. How many enemies do you have in the House of Lords?" Anthony asked.

"A few," said Henry.

"We must go through with Veronica's plan. If a magistrate is there with witnesses when we catch him, the Home Office will wash their hands of him," said Anthony.

"How can you be sure they will not protect him?" Asked Henry.

"I know the man in charge. The Office will not want a scandal that ties them to a criminal. Especially one that has targeted the family of a Marquess," Anthony said confidently.

Henry sat down, rubbing his forehead. "How can the Home Office be entangled with someone like him?" he asked.

"I think they have planted in order to expose him. I can't explain, but I knew the real Parnell," Anthony said in a whisper.

Henry looked up at Anthony with narrowed eyes. "What do you mean 'the real Parnell'?" He asked.

"I met him before I joined the royal navy. Then this fellow showed up, saying he was Parnell. I couldn't say anything because I didn't know how I would explain knowing such a man," said Anthony.

"You're right." Henry said. He stood up and took a deep breath, then said, "Okay, we go with the original plan. But I beg you, please ensure my daughter comes home alive," he said, looking at Ian and William.

"We will," William said. Ian nodded his agreement, then the two of them stood and left the room.

"Henry, I need your silence on this matter. Nobody can know the Home Office is involved in this," said Anthony.

"I assure you I will say nothing. I worry for my daughter and her children. Knowing Parnell has access to such powerful resources is frightening," said Henry.

"Our plan will work. It has too. Now, I must leave. I am expected at Lord Claridge's home for dinner," Anthony said.

"I will see you tomorrow at your wedding," Henry said, smiling.

"Until tomorrow," Anthony said, returning the smile. With a bow, he turned and left the room. On his way to collect his overcoat from the chair where he'd tossed it in his haste to see Henry, he heard footsteps behind him.

"Lord Carlyle, how are you?" Veronica asked, as he turned to see who it was.

"I am doing well. I had some business to discuss with your father," Anthony said. Retrieving his coat from the chair, he slipped it on.

"With everything going on, I haven't congratulated you on your upcoming nuptials," said Veronica.

"Thank you," Anthony said, feeling a smile spread slowly across his face. Just thinking of Ada and their wedding made his heart swell, making it difficult to disguise his happiness.

"You love her," Veronica said more as a statement than a question.

"I believe I might," Anthony said, still smiling.

"What are your plans for after the wedding?" Veronica asked politely.

"I must admit, with everything happening, I have failed to make any plans," said Anthony.

"Oh, dear," Veronica said. She looked away for a second, then smiled at him.

"If I'm not stepping out of bounds... what do you think about bringing Ada to my home in Scotland? It is lovely, and the town nearby has several shops and many places to see. It could be the perfect escape for a newly married couple," said Veronica.

"That is a very generous offer. But may I ask why you would want to do this for us? I know some of what transpired between you and Ada..." Anthony said.

"I have to admit, it is for selfish reasons that I extended the offer. I truly want to be friends with Ada. We never had to opportunity before because we were both caught up in other people's agendas," said Veronica.

"I sincerely believe Ada would love that. I will discuss it with her as soon as our current... situation is dealt with. Thank you, Lady Veronica," Anthony said.

"You are most welcome. I won't keep you any longer. Have a wonderful evening," Veronica said, dipping a shallow curtsy.

"You as well," Anthony said as he bowed.

Veronica watched as Anthony entered his carriage. She thanked God for sending such a man to Ada. She lifted a hand in farewell as the carriage departed, though she knew Anthony could no longer see her. For some reason, she still had a nagging feeling something terrible was about happen.

"Veronica, what are you studying so intently?" Henry asked as he walked up to the front door and stood behind her.

"Father, why do I have such a bad feeling?" Veronica asked, turning to look at him.

"About what?" he asked, wrapping his arms around her.

Veronica laid her head on his chest and his arms tightened the way they used to when she was a little girl, making her feel safe. "I don't know. It's just a feeling I have," she said.

"I will never let anything happen to you or anyone else I love. You know this," Henry said reassuringly.

"I know," she said. She closed her eyes and relaxed, feeling protected in her father's arms.

* * *

When Anthony arrived at the Claridge home, he forced himself to put everything else out of his mind. His parents had also been invited for supper that evening. Ada had been nervous to meet his parents, and although he had not said so out loud, there was good reason for her to be worried. The truth was that Anthony didn't want his father around Ada or Thomas for any length of time. To date he had managed to arrange meetings between their families with only his mother in attendance. Ruth was warm and welcoming, which put Ada at ease.

His fear of the embarrassment his father would likely cause was why he'd been reluctant to introduce him to Ada and her family before now. But he couldn't put it off any longer. When he exited his carriage, his heart sank to see his parents carriage was already there. Once inside, he hurriedly removed his overcoat and gloves and handed them to the butler. "Where are they?" he asked.

"In the dayroom, My Lord," the butler responded.

Anthony walked quickly to the room but then slowed his pace as he entered. His father was standing by the fireplace talking to Thomas, while Ada was seated on the sofa, chatting with his mother and Meredith. Ada looked toward him and smiled when she noticed him come in. His shoulders instantly relaxed as he saw that she was all right.

"Ah, Anthony, right on time," Thomas said as he walked up and held his hand out. Anthony shook it and nodded his head.

Anthony walked over to the ladies, who all got to their feet. Bowing to Meredith, he then leaned forward to kiss his mother's cheek. Next, he turned to Ada, who curtsied, and then allowed him to kiss her chastely on the forehead. His mother smiled to see Ada blush, looking happy at his show of affection. He looked up when he heard his father clear his throat, and could tell he was less than pleased with Anthony's public display of affection. Before anything could be said however, the butler stepped inside the room.

"My Lord. Dinner is served," said the butler.

Anthony stepped between Ada and his mother, gallantly holding out both arms to escort them to the dining room.

As dinner progressed, Anthony noticed his father would not speak to Ada, nor did he so much as look her way. He was grateful his mother had kept Ada occupied in conversation so his father's snub was not so apparent. He desperately wanted this dinner to be over before it became impossible to hold his temper.

Anthony looked over at his mother; she could see her son was growing angry.

"Dear, it is getting late, and tomorrow is a big day for Ada and our son," said Ruth.

"Yes. You are right," Mathew said, pushing back his chair. Taking his cue, Thomas, and then everyone else at the table stood.

"Thank you all for coming. It was a lovely evening," Ada said as they all walked to the door. Anthony's mother walked over to Ada and hugged her.

"I enjoyed our conversation and look forward to many more," Ruth said.

"I would like that," said Ada.

When he and Ruth were ready to leave, Mathew bowed slightly to Thomas. "Lord Claridge, thank you so much for the stimulating conversation," he said.

"The pleasure was mine, Lord Carlyle," Thomas replied with a smile. Mathew did not look at or acknowledge Ada before leaving.

Once the door was closed, Anthony wrapped his arms around Ada. "I apologize for my father's behavior," he said, looking at Thomas over her head.

"I have known your father a long time. I was surprised he acted with as much restraint as he did. Honestly, I had expected to throw him out of the house," Thomas said with a chuckle.

Anthony smiled, tightening his hold around Ada as his own body relaxed.

* * *

Five men stood before Parnell, waiting silently for him to speak.

"Were we able to get someone at the Carlyle's?" Parnell asked, not looking up from the paperwork before him.

"Yes. We have two in the house preparing for the ball, and two in the stables," Maurice said as he walked around to the bookcase behind the men. Parnell sat back and took a deep breath, letting it out slowly.

"Plans have changed, gentlemen. Someone has betrayed me. I am sorely afflicted by it, but I promise to correct things immediately."

Gregory froze. *How did he find out*, he wondered, suddenly finding it difficult to breathe.

Outside the house, a shot rang out. Passersby stopped for an instant to looked around, then hurried on their way. In this part of town, it was best to keep walking and mind one's Ps and Qs.

Chapter Twelve

The wedding day had finally arrived, and Ada was so nervous she felt nauseous. In front of the mirror, Meredith and Ellen finished the final touches to her hair while Eleanor straightened the train of her gown. Ada's dress was a pale green satin with a square neckline and puffy sleeves that stopped just off the shoulder. The bodice was fitted, with intricate flower embroidery and a pearl in the center of each flower. The back was laced down to her waist, where a bow had been pinned to lay flat. The skirt was scalloped and embroidered at the bottom, and was overlaid with a sheer panel. She wore light green gloves that stopped a little above her elbow. Her chestnut hair was pulled up in a Grecian style with a few flowers strategically placed to frame her face. A simple set of pearls hung around her neck—a gift her father had given her the night before.

"You look beautiful," Meredith said as she stepped back to look at Ada.

"You think so?" Ada asked anxiously.

"Yes, Ada, you are beautiful. Anthony will be very pleased," Ellen said.

A tear slipped down Ada's face, causing Meredith to rush forward with her handkerchief. "No crying. Today is a happy day," said Meredith as she wiped it away. She pulled Ada into her arms, careful not to disturb her dress. As the two women embraced, a knock sounded at the door.

Eleanor walked over to open it. "She is ready," she said, stepping back to let Thomas in.

Thomas stood inside the door, unable to stop himself from staring at his little girl. He could not believe how grown up she looked on this, her wedding day. He nodded to the other ladies, then slowly walked up to Ada, and kissed her cheek. "You look beautiful. I am so proud of the woman you have become," he said, beaming.

What little control Ada had over her emotions faded, and her tears began to fall in earnest.

"Oh, sweetheart, don't cry," Thomas said, reaching out to embrace his daughter. He could hear sniffling behind him as the other women reacted to the tender moment.

"Let us be done with the tears," Meredith finally said. She touched Thomas's shoulder gently, and he let go of Ada then stepped back. Meredith used her handkerchief to dry Ada's face, then dabbed a little powder on her cheeks to hide the redness.

"Take a deep breath and let it out slowly," Meredith instructed, demonstrating by taking deep breaths herself.

"I'm okay," Ada said, closing her eyes and breathing deeply.

"In that case, it's time for us to go," Thomas said, proffering his arm to Ada.

* * *

The entrance of Meredith and the other ladies into the church signaled it was time for the ceremony to start. When the music began to play, Anthony emerged from the back room and stepped onto the dais. He was dressed in white breeches, a white shirt with a burgundy cravat, and an embroidered overcoat. He surveyed the guests, surprised at how full the pews were. He noticed his parents sitting close to the front, grimacing inwardly when he saw the smug look on his father's face. Not wanting to let his father ruin his mood, he looked at his mother instead. Her smiling face conveyed enough happiness and love to make him forget his irritation. He smiled back at her with loving affection.

Anthony looked to the doors of the church in time to see his to-be wife walking down the aisle with her father. He was mesmerized by her stunning beauty, and found himself unable to take his eyes off of her. Ada looked up at him halfway down the aisle, and smiled when she saw him watching her.

Although she had been reintroduced to society, Ada still felt uncomfortable being the center of attention. When she saw Anthony waiting for her, her fears vanished. It mattered not who was watching her. Not a soul present could help but notice her love for him, including Anthony. During the ceremony they continued to look only at each other, save for when it came time to exchange rings.

Veronica sat in the front with Sean and her parents. It surprised her that Dinah was there as well, with her parents, Lord Pierce, and Lady Ann. She knew Dinah was still angry at Ada for what Ada and Agnes had attempted to do to her brother and Veronica. Hannah and her parents sat behind Veronica, which also took her by surprise. Perhaps her friends had been forced by their parents to come. It didn't matter why. She was still glad they were there. Looking around, she noticed that her father and Sean were scanning the pews, rather than watching the ceremony. She felt Sean tense when the doors to the church opened to admit a latecomer. Her brother Ellis had returned early from a business trip; he had said it was so that he could attend the ball, but Veronica new it was out of concern for her safety. Everyone was on edge and feeling tense it seemed, herself included.

When the service ended, guests began to leave for the wedding breakfast. As Veronica made her way down the aisle towards the exit, something made her look up to the loft. She noticed a lone figure standing in the corner. Even from a distance, she could tell it was Ada's mother, Agnes. Veronica watched as Agnes wiped away a tear, then turned and disappeared out of sight. She wanted to feel sorry for Ada's mother but couldn't find it in her heart. Agnes has done so many terrible things, hurting so many people. She wondered if Ada knew her mother had been in attendance. Not knowing how Ada felt about her mother, Veronica decided not to mention it for the time being.

* * *

When Veronica and her family entered the Carlyle home, Anthony's father hurried to greet them.

"Lord Cambridge, thank you so much for gracing my humble home with your presence, and for attending my son's wedding," Michael said, bowing low.

"Think nothing of it. Your son is a good man. Besides, Thomas is a dear friend of mine, and Ada has become a friend of my daughter's," answered Henry.

Mathew was stunned, especially by Henry's last statement. For the daughter of such a high-ranking family to become friends with someone in Ada's situation was unheard of. As he struggled to regain his composure, Henry and Ellen congratulated the newly married couple.

"Lord Aldridge, Lady Ellen, welcome," Anthony said.

"Thank you, Anthony," Henry said as they shook hands. Ellen walked over and hugged Ada. Mathew could not believe the familiarity they showed each other. As Henry and Ellen moved on to mingle with the other guests, Mathew turned his attention to the next guests entering his home. He was again speechless as he looked up at the abnormally large man standing before him.

"Hello, Lord Carlyle," said a feminine voice. Mathew looked down to see a woman step out from behind the man. He recognized her as Lord Henry's daughter.

"Ah, Lady Veronica, so glad you came," Mathew said graciously.

"Allow me to introduce you to my husband, Lord McDonald, from the Highlands," said Veronica.

"A pleasure to meet you," Mathew said as he slightly lowered his head.

"Lord Carlyle. It is a pleasure to meet you as well," Sean replied in perfect English. Veronica stared up at her husband in shock. She continued to stare at him as they proceeded through the receiving line, awaiting their turn to congratulate the happy couple.

"We will talk later," Sean said as they moved up and found themselves standing before Anthony and Ada.

"Yes, we will," Veronica said with a smile, then turned her attention to the newlyweds. "Ada, you look beautiful," she said, surprising Ada with a hug.

At the door, Mathew watched the two ladies embrace. He realized that his son marrying Ada was a very good thing. He made a mental note to be friendlier to his new daughter-in-law from now on.

After the meal concluded and good wishes to the bride and groom had been received for the second time, the guests all left to rest and prepare for the ball that would take place later that afternoon. Once inside her carriage, Veronica stared at her husband in silence. Sean had spoken perfect English all day, ignoring his wife's perplexed expression the whole time.

"Ian and Michael helped me learn English," Sean finally explained.

"But why?" Veronica asked.

Sean looked away and took a deep breath, letting it out slowly. "I didn't want to embarrass you," he said, gazing out the carriage window.

Tears welled up in her eyes as she regarded her husband's profile. "Sean, please look at me," she said. She placed her hand on his arm, and he slowly turned his head toward her.

"I married you because I love you," she said. She raised her hands to cup his face, not stopping the tears that fell from her eyes. "I never have, nor will I ever be ashamed to be your wife. You are my Scottish knight—the man who makes me feel safe and loved."

Sean felt an overpowering wave of need for the incredible woman beside him. He reached out to grasp the back of her head, pulling her to him. Leaning his head down, he crushed his lips to hers, entangling his fingers in her hair. Veronica responded in kind, reaching up to encircle his neck with her arms. Each of them poured everything they had into their kiss, communicating without words the depth of love and desire they felt for each other. When they finally separated to catch their breath, Sean leaned forward, touching his head to hers. "I am sorry, lass. I am a daft fool," he said.

Veronica giggled, then lifted her head to look into his eyes. "Perhaps so. But you are my daft fool," she said fiercely.

"Aye that," he said, smiling, then kissed her again.

* * *

Later that afternoon, Anthony knocked on Ada's bedroom door. It opened, revealing her maid, Lucy. Lucy stepped back to allow him in. Entering the room, he found Ada by her dressing table and stopped short. She was now wearing a gown of the same green as her wedding dress. It was low cut and high-waisted, with layers of taffeta and cap sleeves. It was simpler than he expected, but she looked all the more beautiful to him because of it.

"Do I look fitting?" Ada asked, looking down at her dress.

"You look beautiful," Anthony said. He walked up to her and enfolded her in his arms. "I am very pleased, wife," he said.

Ada couldn't help the tears that welled in her eyes at his words. She smiled and said, "Thank you, husband."

Anthony slowly lowered his head and softly kissed her lips. They continued to stare at each other, with love shining in their eyes, long after the kiss had ended.

"We have a house full of guests already," Anthony finally said.

"Then I suppose we would do well to make an appearance," Ada responded, still smiling.

Anthony stepped back to offer her his arm. As he and Ada left the room, the sound of Ada's happy laughter brought Lucy to tears.

Just as they were about to make their grand entrance at the ball, Ada hesitated. Anthony looked down at her, resting his hand on the one she was using to hold his arm. "You need not be afraid. Remember, you are a married woman now. Nobody will ever harm you again," he said reassuringly.

Ada looked up at her husband with gratitude for his comforting words. Then, raising her head high, she nodded to signal her readiness. As they walked into the grand hall, people were already talking and dancing. But when they entered, the music stopped, and the doorman banged his ornate staff upon the floor to command everyone's attention.

"Lord Carlyle and his wife, Lady Carlyle," said the doorman.

Anthony and Ada moved further into the room, and the music began to play again. They made their way through the room, greeting their guests. As they came upon Henry and Ellen, Ada spotted Veronica and her husband beside them talking to her father. They looked to be engaged in a serious conversation, as they spoke quietly with their heads bowed close. Standing beside them Ada saw Lord and Lady Corbin and, to her surprise, Lord Pierce and his wife. What surprised her the most was that Veronica's brother Ellis was in attendance. They all looked uncomfortable, which worried Ada.

When she saw Ada and Anthony, Veronica looked over at them and smiled. Veronica moved closer to them, then threw her arms around Ada again. "Ada, you look radiant. Married life suits you," she said.

Ada suddenly recalled the conversation she had overheard between her father and Anthony, about someone wanting to hurt Veronica. She couldn't believe she had forgotten something so important. Perhaps it explained why everyone around Veronica looked so anxious. "Is everything all right?" Ada asked, directing her question to the group.

"Yes, everything is perfectly fine," her father said, smiling. Ada looked unconvinced.

"I hope everyone is enjoying themselves. Come, sweetheart. We still have guests to greet," Anthony said before Ada could say anything else. He picked up her hand and wrapped it around his arm, then guided her away. Ada looked back once at the group as they walked away. They were no longer smiling, and had already resumed their conversation.

* * *

As the evening progressed, Hannah and Dinah walked over to Veronica during a pause in the music. They were both breathing heavily from the exertion of dancing. Two of the girls prospective suitors, Johnathon, and Oliver, had escorting them from the dance floor. Both men bowed politely when they saw Veronica, then turned to walk away.

"Gentlemen, may I have a word with both of you?" Veronica said, stopping them.

"Of course," said Oliver. The two men followed her to a quiet room, where Sean and Ellis joined them.

"Could we trouble you both with a favor?" Veronica asked.

"Certainly," Johnathan said, looking between Ellis and Sean.

"What's happening?" Oliver asked.

"We need you both to watch Hannah and Dinah tonight," Veronica said.

"Why? Are they in danger?" Oliver asked.

"No, they are not in any danger that we know of. But there are nefarious plans afoot tonight, and we don't want them to become involved accidentally," Veronica said. As she spoke she looked around the room, alert for any threat.

"Do you need our help?" Johnathon asked gallantly.

"No. I am merely concerned that my friends might try to interfere should something happen, and that could cause them to be hurt."

"We will be vigilant in keeping them safe," Oliver said. Sensing the conversation was over, he and Johnathan bowed to Veronica and the other men, then walked away.

"Why did you have to ask *him* to watch Hannah?" Ellis asked, his eyes trained on Oliver as he walked over to where Hannah was talking to her parents.

"Why shouldn't I? He has shown more attention to her than you have. You know Ellis, if you are not careful, he might win the prize that has been right in front of you all this time," Veronica said as she walked off, leaving Ellis staring at Hannah.

* * *

"Is everything ready?" Veronica asked her father a few minutes later.

"Yes," Henry said, worry written on his face.

Sean reached out to grasp her hand, holding it tight. Veronica looked up at her husband with a comforting smile, then looked back at her parents.

"I know you both want to hug me right now, but you cannot because we are being watched. We must not act suspiciously," Veronica said. Henry and Ellen looked chastened. They were both having difficulty concealing their emotions, knowing Veronica would be putting herself in danger.

"It's time," Veronica said, turning to walk away. She found herself unable to, as Sean would not let go of her hand. She looked up at him with exasperation, but her countenance changed as she saw something she had never before seen. There were tears were in his eyes.

"I love you." she quietly mouthed.

"I love ye," he mouthed back, letting her hand go.

Taking a deep breath, Veronica began to make her way out of the grand hall, hoping that to anyone watching it would look like she was headed for the resting room.

Ada had been watching the scene unfold from across the room. She'd noticed the tears in Sean's eyes, and the way he held onto Veronica's hand. She had also observed the worried looks Veronica's parents continued to exchange. As she saw Veronica walk away, she recognized it as an opportunity to talk to her privately. Excusing herself, she told Anthony she would be back shortly.

Veronica proceeded down the corridor slowly. Two elderly matrons walked past her, politely nodding their heads. She continued walking, opening doors from time to time, acting as if she were lost. When she noticed a man unfamiliar to her walk out of one of the rooms, she stopped. Her eyes took in his appearance, noting he was dressed like a stable hand. She immediately sensed this had to one of Parnell's men.

"Pardon me sir. Could you please direct me to the resting room?" Veronica asked sweetly. The man smiled, causing a chill run down her spine.

"Are you Lady Aldridge?" The man asked.

"I was Lady Veronica Aldridge before I married. Why do you ask?" Veronica said.

The man suddenly lunged forward and grabbed her arm, turning her around roughly and pulling her against him. Using one arm to keep her pinned, he pulled out a knife and held it to her throat with the other. "You will come with me and not make a sound," he whispered in her ear.

Moving the knife from her throat to her lower back, he applied enough pressure to prick her back slightly. Then, releasing her briefly, he gave her a push towards the back of the house. As she stumbled, he grabbed her arm, squeezing it painfully. Ada came upon them as they headed toward the rear exit of the house.

"Veronica, can we have a word—" She began, then froze when she saw the man standing behind her. The man was far too close to Veronica, and he had a grip on her arm. She noticed something flash in his hand, but it took her a second to realize it was a knife.

"Ada, go back to the ball immediately," Veronica said firmly. Ada turned to run for help, but stopped when she spied a man, who she presumed was a servant, walking down the hall towards them.

"I need you to inform Lord Carlyle that someone has taken Lady Veronica," Ada called out urgently to the man. Quickly working out a plan in her head, she decided she would run after Veronica and her captor, and would attempt to stall them until her husband and the other men came to rescue them.

"I'm afraid I can't do that, Lady Carlyle," the man said.

"Why ever not? I don't understand. Someone has forcibly taken Lady Veronica," Ada said, getting angry.

"That's because you are going with her," the man said, pulling out a knife. Before Ada could scream, the man pushed her against the wall and covered her mouth.

"If you want to live, you'll shut your mouth and come with me. I was told not to kill you or take liberties with you, but nobody said I couldn't cut that pretty face of yours a little bit," he said as he ran the knife lightly across her cheek. Ada froze. For an instant she was back in the room with Malcolm Randolph, remembering the way he'd held his knife to her face before he raped her. The man pushed her down the corridor. As soon as they were outside, a sack was placed over her head. A push sent her stumbling and she fell to her knees, where she stayed, sobbing. A hand then grabbed her arm and jerked her upright. She was dragged over to a carriage and tossed roughly inside. A man climbed in behind her, and lifted her from the floor of the carriage, placing her none too gently on the seat.

"Don't take that hood off until you are told to," he commanded as the carriage hurriedly took off.

Ada didn't make a sound; she sat frozen in fear, wondering why these men wanted her. She wondered if Veronica was also in the carriage, too afraid to say anything.

Two horses emerged from the alley as soon as the carriage took off. On one horse was William and a young boy; the other carried three more boys. Together they set off in pursuit of the carriage.

Chapter Thirteen

As soon as the carriage took off, Aaron and Ian, who had hidden themselves on the roof of the house, slid down a ladder. Aaron ran into the house, hurriedly making his way into the grand hall. He stopped as he entered the room, searching the crowd. Seeing Lord Aldridge looking his way, he nodded, then retraced his steps down the hall, and waited.

"It's time," Henry said grimly. He kissed Ellen on the cheek before walking away with Sean, Ellis, and Archie. Out in the hall, they approached Aaron, who appeared extremely agitated.

"We need to get Lord Carlyle," Aaron said.

"Why would we do that now? It isn't part of the plan. We don't have time," Henry said impatiently as he began to walk past the man.

"They took his wife," Aaron blurted out, stopping Henry in his tracks.

"What are you talking about? Do you mean Ada?' Ellis asked.

"Yes," said Aaron.

"Go get Anthony," Henry commanded. Ellis immediately took off for the ballroom. Anthony had watched Henry and the others leave, and knew it meant their plan was unfolding as expected. Looking about the room he searched for Ada, nonplussed that he could not find her. When he saw Ellis standing at the entrance of the room beckoning him to come over, something inside his chest tightened. Walking towards Ellis, he could tell something was wrong, and broke into a run.

"Anthony, I have some upsetting news—" Ellis began as Anthony flew past him, not waiting for him to finish his sentence.

"They've taken Ada with them," Henry said when Anthony reached him. He hurried to match Anthony's stride as they made their way out the back entrance.

Anthony couldn't speak for the fear that gripped his heart, and he could barely breathe. Several horses were saddled and ready, but they were one short. Henry and his men had not anticipated Anthony coming with them.

"We don't have time to saddle another. Parnell's men will try to warn him that we're onto them. Anthony, you must ride with Ellis," Henry said as the other men mounted.

"Which way?" Sean asked a man who had materialized from the shadows. The man pointed to his right, and the group took off in that direction. As they came up to a split in the road, a young boy stepped out of the shadows and pointed left. It was very fortunate that Meredith had told Thomas about the orphan boys; she had taken them under her wing and trained them well. Archie threw a small bag of coins at the child as the horses flew past. The boy stepped forward to collect it before racing off.

* * *

When the carriage stopped, Veronica was unceremoniously pulled out. She stumbled to remain on her feet. She'd known someone else was in the carriage with her, and could tell from the sounds she heard that they too, were being roughly dragged out of the carriage. But when Veronica's hood was removed, she gasped to see Ada standing beside her.

"Ada!" She said to her terrified, shaking friend. She reached for her hand, clasping it tightly. Ada did not speak, but Veronica's touch seemed to calm her enough to prevent her from breaking into hysterics.

"Let's go," said one of the men. They grabbed the two women by the arms and pulled them towards a house. Once inside, the women were shoved into an empty room, and the door was shut and locked.

"Ada, you need to stay calm." Veronica said immediately, rubbing her own bruised arms. She walked over to where Ada stood immobile, evidently still in shock. Veronica wrapped her arms around her, but Ada remained silent. "I know this is distressing but you must stay strong Ada. There are people on their way to save us."

Ada stepped back and looked at Veronica with hope in her eyes. "Truly?" She asked.

Veronica nodded. Grabbing Ada's hand, Veronica led her to the back of the room, where they sat on the floor huddled together.

Ada could not help the tears that fell as she thought about how happy she had been such a short time ago. *Is this retribution for the cruel things I did in the past?* she wondered. She thought back to the conversation she'd overheard, when her father and Anthony had discussed a threat to Veronica. Her blood ran cold as she realized how grave their situation was, and she began to shake uncontrollably.

Veronica realized she would have to distract Ada before she became frantic. She knew she had to keep her calm until the men arrived. "Did you know your mother was at your wedding?" Veronica asked, watching Ada's reaction.

Ada raised her head and looked at Veronica with astonishment. "My mother was at my wedding? How do you know?" she asked.

"I saw her in the loft of the church as I was leaving," said Veronica.

"My mother was there?" Ada asked again in a wobbly voice. She began to sob.

Veronica pulled Ada into her arms and let her cry. "I'm so sorry. I didn't mean to upset you more. I was only trying to divert your thoughts," said Veronica.

"No. I am glad you told me. The fact that my mother loves me enough to risk my father's wrath in order to attend my wedding makes me happy," Ada said, wiping her tears.

Both ladies stood quickly when they heard door being unlocked. Ada gasped and stepped back against the wall, staring at her worst fear come true.

Malcolm Randolph stood in the doorway with a smile on his face. "There you are," he said entering the room and closing the door behind him.

Veronica stepped in front of Ada, to obstruct his view. She felt Ada grasp the back of her dress, holding it as if it were a lifeline.

"Malcolm Randolph. What are you doing here? "Veronica demanded.

"I am here to collect what's mine," Randolph answered as he stepped forward.

"I don't believe there is anything in this room that belongs to you," she said. She tilted her head to the side, seeming confused.

"Oh, but there is. Ada, come along," Randolph said calmly, as if expecting Ada to obey him.

Ada tensed and stepped closer to Veronica's back, vainly trying to hide. Veronica looked about the empty room, searching for something she could use to protect herself and Ada against Randolph. She prayed the men would hurry, and arrive before things got further out of hand. Randolph being there without Parnell was a bad sign.

"Sir, are you aware that she has exchanged her nuptials this very day? Ada is a married woman," Veronica said.

"When I am done with her, Carlyle will not want her anymore. Now move aside," Randolph said, walking up to her.

Veronica turned her head to look at Ada. "Let go of me, Ada. You are not going with him, I promise," she whispered. Ada reluctantly let go of her dress. Veronica stepped forward, knowing Randolph would never see her as a threat. "I implore you to forgo this foolishness and leave. There are things going on that you should not be involved in," Veronica said, standing close enough to attack.

"Oh, I am well aware of what is transpiring here. I have no idea what you have done to enrage a man like Parnell, but you have," Randolph said with a sneer. "Now stand aside," he repeated. He reached for Veronica's shoulder, intending to shove her out of the way. Before he touched her however, Veronica swung her fist, catching him square on the chin, causing him to stumble back. A look of shock crossed his face as he stared at Veronica. She had assumed a fighting stance, with fist up and ready.

"I see someone has taught you how to be a pugilist," Randolph said. He laid his cane on the floor and walked toward her. Veronica took another swing, but this time he caught her wrist. She then swung her other fist, which he also caught. Holding both her arms, Randolph looked proud of himself.

"I have been taught many things," Veronica said. Using the tight grip he had on her arms as leverage, she raised her foot and kicked him hard in the chest, sending him flying.

Ada was in shock as she watched Veronica battle Randolph. Though terrified, she absently wondered how Veronica was able to kick him in her dress. Looking at it, Ada realized Veronica's dress was different. There was extra material that overlapped and met in the front to hide the slit that went down both sides of the skirt. Ada's admiration for Veronica increased substantially as she watched her friend. She wished she could be that strong too. She gasped as she saw Randolph get to his feet, his anger evident in the way he brushed off his clothes and bent down to pick up his cane.

"I am afraid Parnell will not get his chance at revenge," Randolph said, his voice cold with rage. He pulled on the bear's head at the tip of his cane, causing it to separate and reveal a hidden dagger. Ada gasped again and moved closer to Veronica, wanting to pull her back away from him.

"I will be all right. Go to the corner so you are not in my way. This won't take long," Veronica said to Ada. She smiled at Ada briefly before turning back to Randolph. But Ada did not move.

"Sir, I implore you to stop right now before you come to harm," Veronica said.

"Oh, I'm afraid it is you who will come to harm," Randolph said stepping closer.

Suddenly Veronica was pulled off balance from behind. At the exact moment Randolph lunged, Ada quickly stepped in front of her. As Veronica regained her footing she stared at Randolph, who seemed frozen in place. Then her heart stopped as she saw the dagger embedded in Ada's side. Veronica reached for Ada as she crumbled to the floor.

"Foolish chit! She should have come willingly, then none of this would have happened," Randolph said as he slowly backed up towards the door.

"SOMEONE HELP," Veronica called out as she held Ada in her arms.

* * *

When Anthony and the other men reached the two-story house, it appeared quiet and empty. Dismounting quickly, they prepared to charge in but heard horses running toward them.

"It's the Magistrate," Ellis said, sounding relieved.

"Excellent. Let's get this bastard," Henry said, already moving towards the house. The other men pulled out their pistols and headed for the door with him. Ian kicked the door open and the men piled in, then stopped short. The house was deathly quiet, which gave them all a bad feeling. It was then that they heard someone yell for help.

"VERONICA!" Sean yelled as he and the other men raced down the hall.

"IN HERE!" Veronica yelled repeatedly, only stopping when they had all burst through the door. Their relief was short-lived as they took in the sight before them.

"Randolph, what the blazes are you doing here?" Henry asked.

"Ada?" Anthony whispered in horror. He ran over to where Ada lay in Veronica's arms. Kneeling beside her, he noticed the dagger stuck in her side. "Ada," he said again, holding her face in his hands.

"I'm sorry," said Ada. She looked at her husband through tear-filled eyes.

"No, sweetheart. It's going to be all right. You're going to be all right," said Anthony.

"What happened here?" The Magistrate asked.

"Randolph has stabbed Ada," Veronica said. She too began to cry.

"It was an accident. The little bitch stepped in the way," said Randolph. Ian and William roughly grabbed him and dragged him out of the room, followed by the Magistrate.

Anthony reached out to pull out the dagger, but Henry grabbed his hand, stopping him.

"No, don't pull it out. We don't know what will happen if you do. Ellis, go fetch the doctor and bring him to Anthony's house. It is the closest place to here," said Henry.

Ellis ran out of the room as Sean knelt down beside Veronica. He was relieved to find her unharmed, but restrained himself from expressing his emotion outwardly with Ada being hurt.

"Sean, please hand me your cravat," Veronica said urgently, looking at her husband. Sean gazed back at her, then looked down, not comprehending what she was talking about. "The cloth around your neck," she said, pointing at it. Sean hurriedly removed it and handed it to her.

"Anthony, come around to this side so you can hold her without disturbing the blade," Veronica said, knowing he would want to hold his wife in his arms.

"Sean, come with me. We must find something we can use to carry her on," said Henry. The two men left swiftly.

Once Anthony held Ada in his arms, Veronica began wiping the blood off her hands, using Sean's cravat. She knew he wouldn't mind; he hated having the thing wrapped around his neck. Veronica then kneeled beside Ada and took her hand. "Ada, why did you do this?" She asked.

"I couldn't let him hurt you..." Ada said weakly. Before she could say anything else, she went limp.

"Ada. Ada, talk to me, please," Anthony said, striving to keep the panic from his voice.

Veronica leaned down and put her head to Ada's chest. "She is still breathing, and her heart is beating strong," she said when she finally raised her head.

Anthony silently prayed for God not to take her away from him as he held her close. He had finally found happiness again. He didn't think he could handle losing another wife he loved. It was then that he realized he truly did love her; he just wished he could tell her how much.

Henry and Sean didn't take long to return with a board about two feet wide and five feet long. It was just big enough to carry Ada. Once they had carefully placed her on the board, they walked out of the room. Anthony remained beside Ada as they moved her, in case she should wake and turn unexpectantly. Veronica followed behind, but when she reached the front door, she froze. The hairs on her arms and neck stood up, giving her the feeling that someone was watching them. She turned around quickly and peered down the hall, but saw nothing. Finally, she turned back to face the door, and left.

The moment Veronica was gone, Maurice stepped out from a dark corner upstairs. He was surprised Ada had been stabbed, but the main thing that needed to happen was for Randolph to be arrested. He knew Feagin would be pleased, but Maurice felt uneasy. Veronica's men had known about Feagin's abduction plot and had set their own trap. He realized there was nothing simple about Veronica Aldridge. She had known someone had been watching them as they left, which unnerved him. He was afraid this vendetta Feagin had against her would end badly. Maurice owed Feagin everything, including his life, and he intended to be loyal to him until one of them ended up dead. He could only hope Feagin would realize this was a fool hearty plan, and change his mind.

Chapter Fourteen

Everyone was quiet as they sat outside the bedroom, waiting for the doctor to come out and speak on Ada's condition. Anthony sat on the floor beside the door. Veronica sat across from him with Ellis and Sean beside her, and Henry watched his children. He was so thankful that nothing had happened to either of them. A noise down the hall made each of them jump; it seemed they were all on edge and uneasy after what had transpired that evening.

"I will go and talk to Thomas," Henry said. He walked down the corridor towards the entrance in anticipation of his friend's arrival. In the chaos, nobody had thought about Thomas and Meredith aside from sending word that they should come immediately.

Ellen noticed Henry approach as she was handing hers and Eleanor's cloaks to the butler. "Why were we sent word to come here?" She asked as Henry took her into his arms.

"Henry, what has happened? We received word that we needed to get here immediately," Thomas said as he helped Meredith remove her cloak.

"Thomas, an unexpected situation came up. They took Ada along with Veronica." Henry said. He released Ellen, then walked up to Thomas.

"My God. That is why we didn't see Ada or Anthony at the end of the ball! We thought they had left early to be alone," Meredith said.

"Where is my daughter Henry?" Thomas asked. Henry could see the color drain from his friend's his face.

"She is down the hall with the doctor," said Henry.

"What happened to her?" Meredith asked. Henry opened his mouth, but Thomas had already taken off down the corridor, not waiting for the answer.

When Anthony saw Thomas, he stood up, not saying anything. Thomas stopped in front of him and looked into his eyes.

"What happened to her?" Thomas repeated in a low voice.

"It was Randolph. He stabbed her." That was all Anthony could get out before tears overtook him. Thomas drew him in for a hug, compassion causing him to set his concern for his daughter aside for a brief instant.

"She is a fighter and she loves you. She won't leave us," Thomas said with tearing rolling down his own cheeks.

Anthony stepped back and took a deep breath, trying to regain control over himself, just as the door opened, and the doctor stepped out.

"She is alive. She'll need complete bedrest for at least a fortnight, and as long as infection doesn't set in, I don't see why she shouldn't make a full recovery," said the doctor.

Veronica closed her eyes and said, "Thank you, God."

"Can I see her?" Anthony asked.

"I gave her some laudanum, and presently her maid is cleaning things up and getting her comfortable," said the doctor.

"I will go and help her," said Meredith, who, along with Ellen and Henry, had followed her husband down the corridor to Ada's room in time to hear the doctor's update. At the door she paused and looked back at the others. "I will come and get everyone when we are finished," she said, then entered the room, closing the door behind her.

"If it's all right, I want to stay the night and watch over her," the doctor told Anthony.

"Yes, of course. My man will show you to your room," said Anthony. As he said this, Anthony's butler stepped out from the corner. "Wilkens show the doctor to his room," he said to the butler.

"It's already been prepared. This way sir," Wilkens said. With a nod, the doctor excused himself and followed Wilkens down the corridor.

"Now, could someone fill me in on what happened?" Thomas asked impatiently, looking from one person to the next.

"Anthony, I believe we could use a good stiff drink for this," said Henry. "Maybe it'll help us figure out what happened ourselves," he added, turning from Anthony to look at Thomas.

"It's this way to my study," Anthony said, leading the way for the others.

Once in the room, the others sat while Henry and Anthony went to the counter to pour drinks. Henry looked up in surprise as two hands reached out to take the drinks he was holding.

"Good God, man, I forgot you were here. You have been unusually quiet," Henry said to Archie.

"I've been deep in thought," Archie said. He crossed the room to hand Ellis and Sean a drink. Henry knew Archie had come up with the plan for how to handle Veronica's abduction. Between the four of them, Archie was the strategist. Henry was the ill-tempered, hot head; Thomas was easygoing, possessing not a single mean bone in his body; and Callum was the underhanded one who liked to pull the strings from behind the curtain. Archie would have made one hell of a military general, but lucky for them, it was not what he had wanted to be. When everyone was settled with their drinks, Henry looked at Archie.

"What do you have planned?" Henry asked.

"First, I need to know exactly what happened. Starting with when they took you from the ball," Archie said, looking at Veronica.

"Everything went as we thought it would. I didn't even know Ada was with me until they removed my hood when we got to the house; I saw her standing there looking so frightened."

Anthony closed his eyes and fought back a fresh wave of tears as he thought of how afraid Ada must have been.

"After we were put in a room, I told her that you would be coming to rescue us. Once she knew this had been planned; she relaxed a little. I told her about her mother being at the wedding in hopes of distracting her," Veronica said.

"Agnes was at the wedding?" Thomas asked, shocked, and then angry.

"Please, don't do anything to Agnes. Ada was so happy to discover her mother still thought about her and that she'd risked so much to see her get married," said Veronica. Thomas took a deep breath, then nodded his head in agreement.

"Please continue," Archie said.

"We heard footsteps and then the door opened. I thought it was Parnell, but it turned out to be Randolph instead. We were both surprised, but for Ada it was more than that. She was beyond frightened. We both knew immediately that he had come for her. I tried to keep him talking at first in hopes that it would give you enough time to reach us, but he was impatient. When things became physical, I handled him well enough until Ada got in between us."

"You fought with him?" Anthony asked, incredulous.

"I assure you my sister can hold her own against even the biggest man," Ellis said proudly. Anthony looked at Veronica with newfound respect.

"Randolph realized that he could not win in a fair fight, and that's when he pulled a dagger. I was ready to disarm him when suddenly I was pulled back and lost my footing, That's when Ada stepped in front of me. It happened so quickly that even Randolph looked stunned. Everything else you will already know, as that was when everyone arrived," said Veronica.

"So, was it Randolph all along?" Anthony asked.

"No, he said while we were talking that he didn't know what I had done to enrage Parnell, but I would pay dearly," said Veronica.

"How did Randolph get involved with Parnell?" asked Ellis.

"It doesn't matter," Archie said, getting everyone's attention. "Parnell will know by now that we have rescued Veronica and Ada. Unless we want him to know that we're aware he still intends to harm Veronica, we must devise an alternate plan."

"What alternate plan?" Henry asked.

"We will say Randolph took Ada and had to take Veronica along because she witnessed what was happening," said Archie. "He will think we are blaming Randolph for the whole thing."

"How do we explain being ready to follow so quickly after Veronica and Ada were captured?" Asked Ellis.

"We will stay as close to the truth as we can. We say that Randolph was obsessed with Ada. He started the rumor about the two of them to ruin her reputation in hopes of forcing Thomas to agree to their marriage. And we were worried he would react badly to Ada's marriage to Anthony, so we devised a plan to protect her," said Archie.

"That will work. It will keep Parnell from knowing we were expecting him," Henry said.

"And it will repair Ada's reputation," Veronica added. "She stepped in front of me to save my life. Randolph admitted that he purposely ruined her. If we do this, it means by the end of the week, Ada will be back in the ton's good graces," said Veronica.

"How do you propose to spread the story quickly?" asked Thomas.

"That is the one thing that Meredith taught me. If you want to spread gossip, say something in front of a servant," Veronica said with a smile.

"This is the story we will use when we inform the magistrate, and it will be what everyone else will hear from us. Agreed?" Archie asked. The others in the room all nodded.

"We need to inform Callum," Thomas said.

"I will do that tomorrow. We will be retrieving Hannah from their home." Archie said. He looked up when he saw Meredith in the doorway. Her entrance caused everyone to rise.

"Ada is settled and resting," Meredith announced.

"Anthony, go ahead," Thomas said, squeezing his shoulder.

After Anthony left, the others informed Meredith of their plans. Meredith thought it was a perfectly splendid idea, resolving to do her part by sharing the story when she and Thomas returned home. Veronica and Ellen both vowed to do the same.

"We must also go home for some rest," Henry said. "Ellen," he said, offering her arm. Ellen walked over to her husband to take it. He turned to Thomas then and said, "The Magistrate will be here in the morning. Please inform him to come to my home when he wishes to speak to Veronica."

"I will," Thomas said with a nod. Then, looking about the room at everyone, he said, "Thank you. All of you."

"No thanks are needed among friends. I would expect the same if it was my daughter," Archie said. Thomas slapped Archie's shoulder, then pulled him in for a hug. Henry struggled to contain his laughter, knowing how uncomfortable Archie was with showing affection. He was surprised when Archie returned the embrace and patted Thomas on his back.

"Please let us know how Ada is faring. If it's all right, I would like to return in a few days to see her," Veronica said as she hugged Meredith.

"Please do. I know Ada would love to see you," said Meredith.

When everyone else had left, Thomas and Meredith went to see how Ada was doing.

"Did you see Agnes at the wedding?" Thomas asked his wife.

"No, I didn't see her. But I was hoping she would come," Meredith said as they reached the door to Ada's room.

Thomas stopped abruptly, looking at Meredith. "You wanted her to be there?" He asked, incredulous.

"Yes. Whether you like it or not, she is Ada's mother. And a girl needs to know that both of her parents love her. Believe me. I would rather Agnes be there than for Ada than to have Ada bear that sort of pain," said Meredith.

Thomas realized then how much it must hurt Meredith not to have the love of her parents. It surely would have hurt her terribly for her to want someone as horrible as Agnes to attend Ada's wedding. "You are right," Thomas said, kissing her on the nose.

"Of course, I am," Meredith said, smiling. Opening the door, they stepped inside and saw Anthony sitting beside the bed, holding Ada's hand.

"How is she doing?" asked Thomas.

"She is sleeping soundly," Anthony said, not looking away from Ada.

"You must get some rest Anthony," Meredith said as she walked over to the chest at the foot of the bed and lifted the lid.

"I am not leaving her side," Anthony said firmly.

"I know," Meredith said, rifling around in the chest. She removed two woolen blankets from it, then closed the lid and laid them on top of it.

"Thomas, would you be a dear and help me move this sofa closer to the bed?" Meredith asked, walking over to one end of the sofa.

"I don't think I can rest," Anthony said in protest when he realized what they were doing.

When the sofa was moved and Meredith had finished covering it with blankets and had placed a pillow at one end, she walked over to Anthony again. "Ada will need you for a few weeks, and you will be of no use to her if you do not take care of yourself. You must at least try to get some rest," she said.

"I can lay down on the bed beside her," Anthony said.

"And what if, in your sleep, you reach out to pull her closer to you? You would not realize you were hurting her," Thomas said.

"You are right," Anthony said, finally seeing the wisdom of their words. He stood and walked over to the couch, sitting wearily.

Thomas added more logs to the fire to keep the room warm, then went over to Ada and kissed her forehead. Walking over to Meredith, who was already at the door, he said, "If anything changes, we will be next door." With that, he and Meredith left the room.

* * *

Across town, Parnell was sitting at his desk when Maurice walked in. "How did things go?" He asked.

"As you hoped—with one unexpected outcome. Randolph stabbed Lady Carlyle," answered Maurice.

Parnell was completely surprised by this. "Wasn't expecting that," he said as a slow smile crept across his face.

"They were expecting something to happen tonight. My man never got a chance to tell Veronica's men that the ladies had been abducted," said Maurice.

"Do you believe someone else betrayed me?" Parnell asked, his smile fading.

"I believe we must be careful and keep our ear to the stone, listening," said Maurice.

"It doesn't matter if they knew ahead of time. At least not as far as us being arrested. I already covered us for that by informing the Home Office that Randolph wanted to abduct Ada.

"But getting to Veronica Aldridge will be difficult." Maurice said.

"Yes. I want you to have the people we have in their homes to be listening closely to anything they say. I want to be informed immediately about anything they hear," said Parnell.

Maurice nodded and then left the room. Parnell turned to look out the window. He thought about what he might do if Veronica's people had learned of his plans to abduct her. *If I cannot go after her, I must find a way to make her come after me*, he thought, smiling again.

Chapter Fifteen

A fortnight had passed, and Ada was healing perfectly. Already she was up and about with an overly attentive Anthony constantly by her side. It took everything Ada could think of to convince him she was fine. She knew he needed to attend to his affairs, and wished him to do so without worrying about her. She was still reeling from the number of get-well letters she'd received. Most of the peerage seemed to have sent at least one. From what Anthony had informed her, it was thanks to the plan Archie and Veronica had come up with.

Some of the ladies of the ton had come by to extend invitations in person. The one that surprised had her most was from Rose. She had sent a letter expressing her desire to stop by to see how Ada was doing. Penelope and Charlotte had also requested an audience, but she had refused them. Ada had agreed to see Rose, but only to find out what exactly was being said about her. To her surprise, it was all favorable, confirming that her reputation had indeed been repaired.

Ada had sent out an invitation to Veronica for dinner, and was relieved when she received an acceptance back. Ada looked forward to the opportunity of thanking Veronica personally for everything she had done.

When Veronica and Sean arrived for dinner, Ada and Anthony were pleasantly surprised to see they had brought little Leah with them.

Anthony walked up to Sean to shake his hand, noticing the little girl in his arms immediately. He was captivated. Leah had raven-black hair that already reached her shoulders, and her mother's sky-blue eyes.. When Leah reached out to him and smiled, Anthony looked to Sean for permission to hold her.

Sean leaned forward to let Anthony reach his arms around her, then take her from him. He watched as Anthony and Leah stared at each other, as though in silent greeting. Leah then began making noises, as if she were trying to talk to him, which made all of them laugh.

"She likes you," Veronica said.

Ada watched and couldn't hide her smile as she thought of him holding their own children.

"He will be an excellent father," Veronica said when Ada began walking towards the drawing room.

"Do ye have a room where she can take a nap," asked Sean as he took Leah back from Anthony. He handed her to the nanny they brought with them.

"Yes. Walter please will show her to the nursery," said Sean.

"Are ye expecting?" Sean asked, surprised they had a nursery.

"Not yet. I still have the nursey from when my first wife was pregnant," Anthony explained.

Sean didn't reply; there was really nothing he could say about that.

When Sean and Anthony entered the drawing room, they found the women already seated comfortably on the sofa. They were talking like long lost friends catching up. It made Anthony happy to see Ada so at ease. The women looked up when they noticed the men come in.

"Leah is being laid down," said Sean as he and Anthony sat in the chairs across from the ladies.

"Good. I am surprised she is still in good spirits after missing her nap earlier. My father does not want to see her go, and spends as much time as he can with her. I feel horrible about returning to Scotland in a few days, but I believe it is the safest place for us right now," Veronica said, glancing at Sean.

"I believe you are correct. We don't know what may happen with Parnell still out there," Anthony said.

"Well, at least Randolph will not bother anyone anymore," Veronica said.

"What have you heard about him?" Ada asked.

Veronica looked at Anthony with surprise. "You haven't told her?" She asked.

"Told me what?" Ada asked, looking at Anthony.

"You have been so happy, I didn't want to bring that bastard's name up and ruin everything," said Anthony.

"I can understand that, and I am happy to hear you have been in excellent spirits," Veronica said. She reached forward to pat Ada's hand.

"Yes, I understand as well. But please tell me, what is going on with Randolph?" Ada said. She held her breath, looking imploringly at Anthony.

"He told the Magistrate the story about being framed by Parnell. The next day they found him hanging in his cell," said Anthony.

"He is dead?" Ada asked with a gasp.

"Yes," answered Anthony.

"Forgive my reaction. It is awful to be glad about someone's life being over, but I just can't help feeling relieved," Ada said. She leaned back on the sofa, visibly relaxing.

"Nonsense, you have every right to feel relieved. No one would think badly about that," said Veronica, which caused Ada to smile at her.

"Thank you for everything you have done for me. My reputation has been restored, and I know I can never repay you for that," Ada said, looking at Veronica.

"You owe me nothing. I want you to be happy," said Veronica.

"That I am,' Ada said. She turned to look at her husband with love in her eyes. She would never forget waking up that first night after she was injured, finding Anthony beside her, holding her hand. When he saw her eyes flutter open, he'd been overjoyed. With tears shining in his eyes, he'd told her how much he loved her, and how afraid he'd been when he thought he might lose her.

"The invitation still stands by the way," Veronica said.

"What invitation?" Ada asked, looking puzzled.

"I completely forgot after everything that happened," said Anthony. "Veronica has invited us to come and spend a week at her castle in Scotland," he said.

"Truly?" Ada asked with wide eyes.

"Yes," Veronica said, laughing.

"I would be honored," said Ada.

"Then it is settled. Once you are completely healed, and you have time, you will come and stay for a week," said Veronica.

"The hunt is coming up soon. Ye might enjoy it," Sean said, looking at Anthony.

"Yes. I've heard many good things about it," said Anthony, his eyes and voice exuding excitement for an instant. Then he quickly looked at Ada. "That might not be the most romantic thing to do after just being married," he said.

"Nonsense. There is nothing more wonderful than watching one's husband be the hunter," said Ada. She smiled brightly at Anthony.

"Then it is settled. Everyone will come for the hunt. We will send word when the exact date is arranged," said Veronica.

The rest of the evening was perfect. Ada could not have been happier, and Anthony found himself unable to take his eyes off of her. She was so beautiful, and her laughter and pleasant countenance made her even more so. He too recalled the night when she had first awakened after being stabbed, and how he'd expressed his love for her. He remembered how much she'd cried to hear his tender words. Each night since, he'd gotten on his knees and thanked God for what he had been given, and for the life that was yet to come.

* * *

Feagin was reading through a file at his desk while Maurice sat down in front of him.

"This is her only close acquaintance?" Feagin asked, as he read.

"Yes. She only has two close friends other than her family," said Maurice.

"Hannah Corbin, daughter of Viscount Archibald Corbin. What have you learned about her?" Feagin asked.

"Rumor has it she is in love with Ellis Aldridge. Other than that, nothing out of the ordinary," Maurice said.

"Do they think there will be a match?" Asked Feagin.

"It is more than likely," said Maurice.

Feagin reached over and picked up a different file. Maurice recognized it as the one on Ellis Aldridge. As Feagin sat back to read, Maurice noticed a distant look come into his eyes. Maurice knew it meant he was planning something. He watched Feagin stop and write something down on piece of paper, moving on to read the next set of papers.

"Dinah Pierce, daughter of Callum Peirce, Earl of Westridge. Tell me about her," Feagin said.

"Her brother was Lady Veronica's first husband. You know how that ended. She is known as a daughter of the first water," said Maurice.

"Is she that beautiful?" Feagin asked, looking up from reading.

"I went to see for myself; she is very beautiful," said Maurice with a nod.

Feagin sat back silent for a moment. "Were you able to get their schedules?" He finally asked.

"Yes, but only for the upcoming month. The season is halfway over, and neither girl goes to very many social events during the fall," Maurice said, handing Feagin a piece of paper.

Feagin read it over, then raised his head to look a Maurice. "Dinah Pierce is to attend Lady Westmoreland's weekend tea party," he said. Maurice says nothing, only nodding his head. Feagin wrote something else on the paper, then handed it to Maurice. "Find me these two people," he said.

Maurice read the names, then looked up in surprise. "Robert Westmoreland?' He asked.

"Yes. He is supposed to be on a ship to France, but I know for a fact you will find him in one of the brothels," said Feagin. Maurice said nothing, making no move to leave. He could only stare as he processed what Feagin had told him.

"You don't approve." Feagin said when he noticed the look on Maurice's face,

"Are you sure you want to do this? That girl has done nothing to deserve him," said Maurice.

"I don't relish using a beast like Westmoreland, but I need Veronica Aldridge to be mad enough to come to me," said Feagin. Maurice rose slowly, then left the room.

When the other man was gone, Feagin turned and stared out the window, unable to suppress his smile. "Soon, you will come to me, and I will make you pay," he said.

* * *

Two months had passed since their dinner with Veronica and Sean, but Anthony and Ada were finally on their way to Scotland.

"Is this it?" Ada asked as their carriage stopped in front of a country cottage. they exited the carriage.

"I believe so," Anthony said as he took her hand to help her exit the carriage. He could see she was nervous. "She will be happy to see you," he added.

Ada looked up at him and nodded her head. As they walked up the stone walkway to the door of the cottage, Ada spied a beautiful garden in the distance. She noted there were roses planted by the house, and they looked well cared for. *At least my father didn't leave her in squalor,* she thought.

Before they could knock, they heard someone say, "Can I help you?" Looking to their right, they saw a tall man dressed as a gardener approaching.

"Is this where Agnes Claridge lives?" Ada asked the man.

"Yes," the man answered as he came to stand before them. "You must be her daughter Ada," he said.

"How do you know who I am?" Ada asked.

"She described you perfectly. I am John Hammond—her husband," the man said. Ada and Anthony both looked stunned.

Anthony regained his composure first. "We didn't know she had remarried. I am Anthony Carlyle, Ada's husband," he said, holding out his hand.

"She is not the same person you once knew. I hope you have come because you miss her, not to cause her stress," John said, looking at Ada. "She has paid her dues, and does not deserve further punishment," he said.

"We mean no harm. Ada only wanted to talk to her," Anthony said.

John nodded his head and walked up onto the step next to them, then opened the door. "Agnes, you have guests," he called as they entered.

It is a nice little cottage. Very clean and well furnished. Ada thought with relief. It seemed her mother had done well for herself.. She turned to see her mother coming out of what looked to be the kitchen, then froze. She did not recognize her mother—in fact, she could have walked past her on the street and not realized it. Gone was the haughty, arrogant woman she'd known her whole life. In her place was a commoner. Agnes wore a plain grey dress, with an apron wrapped around her pregnant belly.

"Ada?" Agnes said as tears fell from her eyes.

"Mother," Ada said, her voice choked with emotion. Ada ran to her, and the two women wrapped their arms around each other and cried.

Finally, Agnes stepped back and held Ada's face in her hands. "Oh, my beautiful little girl. I am so happy to see you," Agnes said. She began to cry harder. "I am so sorry for everything I've done. Can you forgive me?" She asked, then bent over and held her stomach. John went ran to her, helping her to a chair.

"Are you okay, my beloved?" He asked with concern.

"I am fine," Agnes answered.

"Are you sure you are, okay? I didn't mean to cause you pain," Ada said. She knelt down in front of her mother.

"No, I am not in pain. I am so happy to see you," Agnes said.

Ada stood up and held out her hand to Anthony. "I wanted you to meet my husband," she said.

"It is a pleasure to meet you," Anthony said as he bowed his head.

"I am so happy Ada found a good man to marry," Agnes said to him, then turned back to Ada. "You were a beautiful bride," she added.

"I was so happy when Veronica told me you were there," said Ada.

"I was very surprised to see her there, but then again, she was always a good person," Agnes said, looking down.

"Veronica has been very good to me. She helped me when I needed it the most, and for that I will be forever grateful. But I didn't come here to talk about her. I want to hear everything that has happened with you. It appears I am going to have a brother or sister soon," Ada said with a smile.

"Yes. In a little over a month. Let's go into the receiving room and sit," Agnes said. She allowed her husband to help her up.

"I will bring some tea," John said once Agnes was seated.

"How did you meet your husband?" Ada asked when John had left the room.

"I was working as a cook in the tavern not far from here. He would come in every day and try to talk to me. Initially, I did not pay him any attention, but he continued to return each day. I finally gave him a chance. He has shown me what real love means," Agnes said. Ada could see the love in her eyes. "It wasn't long after we were married that I became pregnant. We both worry about being parents so late in life but can't be happier," Agnes finished.

Ada looked at Anthony, and they both smiled. "We have news also. I too am pregnant. You are going to be a grandmother," Ada said.

Agnes held out her hand for Ada to take. "You have brought such happiness to me, Ada. I don't deserve your forgiveness or love. But I want you to know I love you with all I have," Agnes said.

Ada bent down and hugged her mother. When John returned with tea, they sat and talked for hours.

"It is getting late. Would you like to stay the night? We have an extra room. It is simple but clean," John asked, hoping they would stay. Their visit had removed much guilt from Agnes, and he loved seeing her smile.

Ada looked at Anthony, who smiled back at her. "It is up to you. We are not expected to be in Scotland for a few more days," he said.

"Then we would love to stay the night," Ada said with a smile. She loved seeing her mother's eyes light up.

"You are headed to Scotland?" John asked.

"Yes. I was invited to participate in a large hunt," Anthony said.

"I have heard of a hunt that happens up there at a castle," said John.

"Veronica's castle?" Agnes asked.

"Yes, "Anthony replied.

"I am glad you have her as a friend. You need good people in your life," Agnes said to Ada.

After supper, John showed Anthony the garden as Ada and Agnes cleaned the kitchen. Ada told her mother about everything she had missed, including the news about Malcolm Randolph's death. Later that night, Anthony and Ada lay in bed discussing the day. Ada still could not believe that her mother was remarried and pregnant—or that she was taking care of the household herself. "It seems my mother found more happiness in being humble than she ever did as a member of high society," she said.

"I must agree with you. She has found happiness. Did your mother say anything to you about the baby?" Anthony asked.

"What about the baby?" Ada asked.

"When John and I took a turn in the garden, he asked me to promise that if anything happened to him or Agnes, that would we take care of the baby," said Anthony.

Ada's head popped up from his chest and she turned to look at him. "What did you say?" She asked.

"I said, of course, we would. The baby will be your little brother or sister," said Anthony.

"Thank you. You make me feel so blessed. I have found the perfect husband and I love him dearly," said Ada.

Anthony kissed her head. "I love you too," he said.

"I am glad we did this. I wasn't sure at first if this was the right thing to do, but after spending time here with my mother and her new husband, I wouldn't change a thing," said Ada.

"That makes two of us," Anthony said as he looked down at his wife. He watched her as she drifted off to sleep, a smile upon her face.

Milton Keynes UK
Ingram Content Group UK Ltd.
UKHW020413240824
447344UK00004B/515